Minced, Marinated, and Murdered

ALSO BY NOËL BALEN
(with Jean-Pierre Alaux)

THE WINEMAKER DETECTIVE SERIES

A fun made-for-TV mystery series that takes
readers deep into French wine country.

Treachery in Bordeaux
Grand Cru Heist
Nightmare in Burgundy
Deadly Tasting
Cognac Conspiracies
Mayhem in Margaux
Flambé in Armagnac
Montmartre Mysteries
Backstabbing in Beaujolais
Late Harvest Havoc
Tainted Tokay
Red-Handed in Romanée-Conti
Requiem in Yquem

www.lefrenchbook.com/winemaker-detective-series/

Minced, Marinated, and Murdered

A Gourmet Crimes Mystery

Noël Balen and Vanessa Barrot

Translated by Anne Trager
Adapted by Amy Richards

First published in France as *Petits meurtres à l'étouffée* by Noël Balen and Vanessa Barrot

©Librairie Arthème Fayard, 2014
English adaptation: ©2018 Le French Book

First published in English in 2018
by Le French Book, Inc., New York
www.lefrenchbook.com

Translation: Anne Trager
Adaptation: Amy Richards
Translation editor: Amy Richards
Cover: HOKUS POKUS CRÉATIONS
Photo: ©Taonga/Fotolia. Kai Keisuke/Shutterstock

ISBNs
Trade paperback: 9781939474674
E-book: 9781943998029

Cooking is the most ancient of the arts,
for Adam was born hungry.
—Jean-Anthelme Brillat-Savarin

Prologue

The rhythmic thud of the knife hitting the wooden cutting board was the only sound in the kitchen as Clotilde Bizolon chopped turnips well before sunrise. The sound dulled her heartache, helping her make it to dawn. She picked up the pace with the rutabagas, a perfect addition to her soup and stew—a soldier's comfort food, filling his belly and keeping him going.

Clotilde smoothed her apron and examined her simmering pots. She contemplated how she would make the bread and canned milk stretch as far as possible, along with the small sausages donated by the neighborhood butcher and the Beaujolais bottled by the area's vine-growing farmers.

Since losing her husband and son, Georges, in the war, one thing kept her going: the makeshift counter she had set up, with the help of some Lyon residents and an American benefactor to hand out free lunches to the young servicemen streaming into the Perrache train station. It was little more than a few wooden planks on barrels. That didn't matter. They did the job. Thousands of fine young men were going off to the front, and many were coming back crippled and demoralized. They deserved a warm greeting, a nourishing lunch, and a glass of wine or cup of real coffee, a great improvement over the chicory tablets in their backpacks.

Perhaps after the war she would open her own restaurant, like Françoise Fillioux, who had a place on the Rue Duquesne. The shop where Clotilde's husband had repaired shoes was going unused, and she needed to support herself. Cooking was something she knew how to do. Her mother had taught her all the region's simple and satisfying dishes made with fresh fish, Bresse chickens, goat cheese, sausage, and frog legs. Clotilde was confident she could run a business on a shoestring.

"Who knows?" she said to herself as she wiped off her cutting board. "The newspaper ran a photo of my stand at the train station. Maybe when the war's over they'll be writing about my restaurant. 'Madame Bizolon's rich and succulent chicken with truffles and elegant quenelles…'"

Clotilde chuckled. At heart she was a modest woman. Still, she was gratified by the recognition her stand was getting. And it certainly had helped her raise the money and supplies she needed.

How far down the road a restaurant venture would be, no one could predict. For now, France was at war, and she had a mission.

Clotilde finished packing everything for the trip to the Perrache station. The sun was up, and the first train from the front would be pulling in shortly. The troops would spill out of the cars, haggard and hungry.

She gave her son's photo on the fireplace mantel a last look. In his short life, Georges had never given her a moment's trouble. "I hope I'm making you proud, son. Give your father my love. Tell him to be patient. I'm not planning to join him anytime soon." She patted her hair in place before opening the door. There wasn't a cloud in the sky. She let the sun warm her cheeks for a moment and then set off to feed her boys.

1

The last diners, a couple in their fifties, stepped out of the restaurant. Holding hands, they strolled into the night. The hour was late and the lights of Lyon were flickering. Jerome Thevenay locked the front door and lowered the metal shutters. The Petit Pouce was now hidden from the street.

The intruder had slipped into the dark kitchen minutes before the restaurant closed and was watching in the shadows as Jerome turned off the coffee machine, sponged the zinc countertop, corked a bottle of Grand Marnier, and put away the stemware, still steaming from the dishwasher. The drainboard was empty, the stove scrubbed down, and the floor washed. Jerome took one last look around before heading toward the dining room.

But the smell! How could he miss it? The kitchen reeked of the burned oil he used to fry onions for his so-called traditional *foie de veau*. He should have used butter—nothing but clarified butter—to sauté the calf's liver and caramelize the onions. Instead of following his grandmother's perfectly fine recipe, deglazing with red-wine vinegar and sprinkling with chopped parsley, he had used olive oil, balsamic vinegar, and whole handfuls of parsley!

The intruder tiptoed closer to the dining room, where Jerome, a checked dish towel thrown over his shoulder, was wiping off the blackboard. Jerome picked up a chunk of white chalk and wrote out the next day's menu in round letters:

Starters
Pistachio sausage en brioche
Eggs en cocotte with crayfish

Main courses
Tripes à la lyonnaise
Ragoût d'agneau

Desserts
Bugnes
Pumpkin tart

One price covered the starter, main course, dessert, and a glass of Beaujolais, coffee and tip included. He reread the board several times before putting it down on an easel.

Then he walked into his office and settled into the big leather chair behind his desk.

His back was to the door. Perfect.

Jerome took his time as he counted the bills, change, and credit card receipts. They weren't bad for a weekday. He arranged the receipts and did a recount, tapping the figures into a handheld calculator before copying them in his bookkeeping ledger the old-fashioned way. He scribbled something on a notepad—probably a things-to-do list for the next morning.

He wouldn't be needing it.

Jerome checked the numbers a final time, oblivious to the sound of shuffling behind him.

It was too easy. As soon as the rolling pin smashed into his skull, he slumped to the side of his chair, his head oozing blood. Pulling him to the tile floor and trussing him was almost as simple as whipping up an omelet.

When Jerome regained consciousness, his confusion transformed to terror. He fought to free his hands and legs. No good. A thick rope around his neck secured the garbage bag that had been yanked over his head. Panicked, he struggled for air. Was he thinking of plans for his restaurant that would never come to fruition, or how his wife and children would get by without him, or perhaps whether there was a heaven or hell? Who would ever know? The bag stopped heaving. Jerome Thevenay was brain dead in six minutes.

2

They were no longer in the countryside, but not quite in the city either. Here and there, wisps of chimney smoke were rising in the pale gray sky. Rows of suburban houses were springing up. And then a mall came into view, followed by clusters of buildings and warehouses. In less than ten minutes, the bullet train would screech into Lyon's Part-Dieu station, pouring out herds of passengers numbed by its tranquillizing sway.

Once on the platform, the middle managers would put on energetic faces and smooth the wrinkles from their suits, while the entrepreneurs would lift their chins to go conquer the world. The morning shuttle linking Paris to Lyon carried few happy-go-lucky tourists and even fewer large families. It was time for work and success.

Murmuring rose in the compartment as the train slowed. Passengers closed their laptops and stowed their magazines.

Paco Alvarez got up and rolled his stiff shoulders before walking to the baggage rack near the exit. A man in a gray three-piece suit was staring at him. Paco knew his camouflage parka, rough-cut jeans, Mexican boots, and three-day shadow made him stand out in this crowd. He smiled at the suit wafting rosemary and lemon aftershave and grabbed the backpack holding his cameras and lightboxes. He swung a bag containing a dozen lenses over his shoulder and picked up the long case where he kept his tripod and white canvas umbrella. As he made his way to the still deserted gangway, he trailed behind him a small suitcase in which he had tossed his computer and a few clothes. Paco didn't like cluttering the aisle with his equipment.

He glanced back at the woman who had been sitting next to him on the train. Laure Grenadier was still seated, rereading, he assumed, the article on wok cooking she had been talking about. Apparently, it was becoming regional, at least in the United States. A chef in San Francisco was creating wok dishes with sourdough and quails from a Bay Area provider, and two chefs in Austin, Texas, were using beef brisket.

"I don't like the jostling while everyone debarks," Laure, her eyes fixed on the article, had told him when he rose from his seat.

Paco leaned his forehead against the cool windowpane and savored the moment of solitude. Laure was the smartest and sexiest boss he had ever encountered. But the woman never quit working. It wasn't just wok cooking that she had gone on and on about during their train ride to Lyon. She had exhausted him with her detailed descriptions of Lyon's traditions and highlights.

He'd made the mistake of admitting ignorance. All he'd done was ask what a *bouchon lyonnais* was, and she had served up more information on the city's trademark restaurants—with their distinctive décor, duck pâtés, roasted pork, sausages, and the like—than he cared to know. According to Laure, Lyon boasted scores of certified bouchons and many others that described themselves as bouchons.

Paco understood why Laure, already an acclaimed food writer by the time she was twenty-five, had skyrocketed in the ranks to become managing editor of *Plaisirs de Table* magazine. Her eyes glistened with passion as she leaped at the opportunity to explain the origins of Lyon's bouchons, which evoked the friendly smoke-filled atmosphere of long-ago inns.

"But why are they called bouchons?" Paco had asked. "That's the word for cork. Was it because they kept popping open bottles?"

Laure smiled. "Not a bad theory. But no, Beaujolais wine had nothing to do with it. Nobody exactly knows the origin of the name. Although it's probably untrue, I like the theory that the name comes from the sixteenth-century word for the packets of straw used to wipe down the horses that were stabled in Lyon overnight. Lyon was once a rest stop for travelers making their way between the Alps and the Massif Central. People would stop to eat, sleep, and have their horses tended to."

"Okay, but why would an innkeeper name his business after a handful of straw?"

"Well, the innkeepers would hang a bundle of straw on the door, and over time it came to symbolize places that offered good food."

Laure had then explained some of the traditional dishes served in bouchons. As humble as the food seemed, Paco salivated at the mention of *tablier de sapeur*, breaded and fried tripe named after the leather aprons French firefighters once wore. He laughed at the etymology of *cervelle de canut*, which meant silk-weaver's brain. Silk had made the city rich, and apparently the weavers had loved the soft herb-filled cheese. Paco's stomach even let out a noisy feed-me rumble when she described artichoke thistles served with bone marrow.

He would like Lyon, no doubt about it. Born just outside Madrid, Paco had immigrated to France, Paris specifically, when he was twenty and had become thoroughly enamored with the country's rich and diverse cuisine. The importance every French citizen accorded to the pleasures of eating inspired him almost as much as the classic dishes themselves. But this was more his style— humble, reminiscent of the rustic *cocido* stews, the simple rice dishes, and the *bocadillo* sandwiches of his youth. He looked forward to his discoveries in Lyon, even at the risk of adding to the padding around his waist that he'd noticed recently.

The train finally rolled to a stop, and he was the first to hop on the platform. He watched the other passengers parade by before spotting Laure, the last to debark, as expected. *¡Dios Mío!* She looked fine in that black and gray outfit: fitted leather jacket, skinny jeans, designer scarf, cashmere sweater, and ankle-boot heels. Parisian through and through.

The photographer looked down at his baggy jacket and pants. Although Laure was too classy to say anything disparaging about his appearance, the two of them were clearly from different worlds.

They ferried their baggage under the concrete arches of the train station, emerging on a plaza where they found a taxi stand on the left. After several minutes, a taxi approached, the driver's-side window down despite the cool autumn temperature. The balding driver gave them a nonchalant look-over before nodding toward the door.

A local radio station played nondescript jazz as they rode through the bleak and angular Part-Dieu neighborhood. They crossed the Rhône River and then the Saône River. Paco was taking it all in when the news came on. Northeast of the city, a demonstration organized by striking workers was expected to block traffic. A spokeswoman for the National Opera talked briefly about the upcoming evening's program, *Mozart and Salieri* by Rimsky-Korsakov, and then there was a short piece on how climate change was affecting the grape harvest. Just as Paco was beginning to tune it all out, an unexpected silence caught his attention. Two seconds later the news anchor cleared his throat.

"This just in," he said, his voice grave. "Jerome Thevenay, owner of the Petit Pouce, a well-known bouchon on the Rue Saint Jean, has apparently been slain in what sources say could have been a robbery. A staff member discovered Thevenay's body and told police that money was missing. The police are at the scene, and we'll keep you updated as soon as we have more information."

Paco turned to Laure. He was about to ask if she had ever met this bouchon owner, but the look on her face stopped him.

"No," she said, letting out a sob. "It can't be."

Paco took her hand and held it gently. She had answered his question.

3

Canary yellow crime-scene tape girdled the Rue Saint Jean. As the lights of the police cruisers bounced off the façades, Laure and Paco elbowed their way through the tight crowd on the Place du Change. They got stuck a few meters in. All around, bystanders were speculating. One man was convinced that a customer had staked out the restaurant and returned to murder the owner after closing. Another mentioned an argument between Jerome and the proprietor of a nearby establishment. A short woman in an Astrakhan cardigan suggested an affair that had turned sour, while some wondered if one of the neighborhood's homeless people had done it.

Laure's stomach was queasy. She tapped Paco's arm, indicating they should go back. It served no purpose to just stand there, subjecting themselves to the stench of the herd. But no sooner had they started heading in the direction of their hotel than Laure spotted a familiar face. It belonged to a tall, lean man who was pushing his way out of the crowd. Nodding to Paco, she quickly skirted the safety barrier to reach the Rue de la Loge.

"Tony?" she asked, not quite sure of herself when she got closer. She took two more steps in his direction. Now there was no question. "Tony!"

The man picked up his pace, looking over his shoulder as if being pursued. Then he stopped in his tracks and turned around. Showing no sign of surprise, he waited for Laure to reach him at the corner.

"Have I changed that much?" she said when she finally got there, with Paco trailing behind. "Didn't you recognize me?"

"Of course I did," Tony said in a low voice.

Seeing the anxiety in his eyes, Laure suggested that they move. As they hurried away from the commotion, she introduced Paco, who extended his hand. Antoine Masperas, aka Tony, simply nodded. He had a battered face with the sunken cheeks and flat nose of someone who had taken as many punches as he'd given.

Laure had known Jerome Thevenay's *commis de cuisine* for a long time. Although they had never been close, she respected this unpolished, taciturn, and sensitive man who bore the stigmata of a dozen years in the Foreign Legion. He'd seen the world and all the violence, poverty, terror, and heartbreak it had to offer. Then, exhausted, he had hung up his stripes and returned home—not far from here, on the hill that led to the Saint Jean Fort. He had worked a few odd jobs to resume a normal life and had finally found his place in the kitchens of the Petit Pouce.

"What happened?" Laure asked.

"I was the one who called the cops," Tony said.

"Were you the first one there?"

"Got in at ten, like usual, to do the prep."

"How awful!"

"I've come across my share of stiffs. But this was different. He was my friend."

Laure saw his jawline tighten. She could sense the rage. A life of challenges and hard knocks had taught Tony how to contain his violence, but only barely. Despite everything, he had made it through, thanks to sheer will and an occasional show of grace. Jerome Thevenay had been one of those godsends. He had held out his hand, and Tony had seized it.

The two of them had grown up together and had shared memories of throwing snowballs, sliding down hills on makeshift sleds, and engaging in neighborhood fights for a handful of marbles. Jerome had been his friend—maybe his only friend—and certainly one for whom it was worth making something of himself.

"The bastards tied him up and suffocated him in a garbage bag!"

Laure, fearful that he might lash out instinctively or collapse in sobs, checked an urge to reach over and console him. She waited while he collected himself. "Was it one person, or were there were more?" she asked.

"I don't know," he said, wiping his forehead with the back of his hand. "The place was robbed. The cops grilled me. It stinks. They're trying to nail this on me."

"Don't worry, Tony. They're only doing their job. You discovered the body. They're making sure they have everything they need. I'm sure they're questioning other people just as intensively."

"I know the cops. I've got a record. It's not pretty, either. When they find out..."

"Serious crimes?" Paco asked.

Tony shrugged. "Petty stuff. I used to lose my cool over anything. I got a suspended sentence for beating up some asshole who cut in line at a movie theater."

"I'd say that's being a bit hot-headed," Laure said.

"Petty stuff, I told you. I was young and had a chip on my shoulder."

"But that's history, right?" Paco asked.

Laure glanced at Paco. He was fidgeting, obviously nervous, as she had been a few minutes earlier.

"I did six months for stealing mopeds. When I got out, I dealt hash and fooled around with stolen checks. After that, I ran off to the Legion."

Tony looked back at the crowd on the Place du Change. "I waited too long to call the cops."

"That was a mistake," Laure said. "You should have done it right away."

"Yeah, you're right."

"They'll be calling you in for more questioning."

"I'm sure. But I've got to get away from here and clear my head first. I'm not going back to the slammer. No way."

Laure didn't respond. Tony, battered by life and saved by an old friend, was delusional. He had never been in charge.

4

Laure and Paco watched as Tony crept away along the embankment of the Saône River. When he had disappeared under the trees, Paco spoke up. "*¡Joder!* What a funny guy."

"I don't like seeing him like that," Laure said. "He's not a bad person, but you never know how he's going to react. And to think I promised you a cushy assignment. You haven't been here more than a few hours, and somebody's already been murdered."

"You've got a point. You said Lyon embodied the *art de vivre*. I can go back to Paris to come across folks getting murdered." Paco rummaged in his pocket and pulled out a pack of gum. He offered a stick to Laure, who declined, before unwrapping one for himself and popping it in his mouth. "So you really think Thevenay's commis had nothing to do with your friend's death? For an innocent person, he was wound tight."

"I think he was telling the truth, Paco. He was devoted to Jerome, and with his background, it stands to reason he'd assume the worst. Of course, he does have a temper... Laure shook her head. "Bottom line, I just don't see him murdering Jerome."

"And you've never been wrong about anyone?"

Laure ignored the question and suggested returning to the Hôtel des Artistes, where they had dropped off their bags without seeing their rooms. They'd been in a hurry to get to the scene of the tragedy.

As they walked, Laure explained that she had known Jerome for many years. In fact, he was one of the few restaurant owners whom she considered a close friend. They'd met when she was working as a freelancer on her first assignment outside Paris. She couldn't imagine the pain his wife, Chloe, and their two children, Jules and Marie-Anne, were feeling. His sister also had to be in a bad state. "What a disaster! I still can't believe it."

When they arrived at the Place des Célestins, they entered the hotel and apologized for their earlier haste. The receptionist took their names.

"What was that again?" she asked Paco.

"Ermenegildo. I was named after my grandfather," Paco said, aware that the French had a hard time rolling the *r* under the tongue and then ripping a *jota* from the back of the throat. "You can call me Paco. It's easier." He grinned at the receptionist.

She blushed and rushed off to find their bags.

"Such a Latin lover," Laure said. "I'm guessing that works all the time."

"Let's just say I don't go unnoticed."

They went to their respective rooms to freshen up, agreeing to meet in the lobby in a half hour.

Paco had barely descended the steps, after brushing his teeth and putting on a clean shirt, when Laure announced a change in their plans: "I've rethought our schedule. We're going to see Gilles Mandrin right away. He runs Au Gros Poussin, and he was Jerome's best friend. It's the least I can do."

She headed toward the door, not waiting for a response. Six paces behind, Paco couldn't help but admire the way she made time in the black stilettos she had changed into. And the seven-centimeter heels showcased her long curvy legs.

"So who is this Gilles Mandrin, besides being another restaurant owner and a friend of our murder victim?" he asked, catching up with her on the sidewalk.

"I'm not really close to him," Laure said, keeping her stride. "He's one of the more colorful characters on the Rue Mercière. But I've always admired his work, his hospitality, and his menus."

"Tell me more."

"Mandrin's a bon vivant with pink cheeks and spiky blond hair. He has the paunch of a man intent on squeezing every drop out of life without trying to understand its meaning."

Paco noted Laure's signature way of talking—passionate, descriptive, and instructive. In effect, she was telling him how to capture the people and atmosphere of Lyon with the eye of his camera. He listened attentively.

"He's a pleasure-seeker with very high standards. He's always looking for something new."

"Where does he get that?" Paco asked.

"He was an adored middle child. I think he always felt like his mother's favorite, and nobody objected when he inherited the family business. He changed the name to Au Gros Poussin."

"You mean like 'cock of the walk'?"

"Apparently it was his nickname when he was a kid."

Paco couldn't help smirking. He'd see for himself.

In five minutes they had reached the Rue Mercière and pushed open the restaurant's heavy nail-studded door. They found Gilles Mandrin in the large dining room.

But this was hardly the spirited man Laure had described. Mandrin's eyes were red and puffy, his skin waxy, and his cheeks sunken. Even his round belly seemed to sag, as if yesterday's strapping torso could no longer hold it up. The stalwart shoulders, deprived of their strength, had renounced any arrogance.

Mandrin remained still for an instant, as if paralyzed by the food editor's arrival. Then he slipped around the counter and enveloped her in his arms.

"It's good to see you," he said, sniffling. "Darn, darn, darn! Jerome was one hell of a guy."

Mandrin's embrace swallowed up the tiny woman. She turned her head to free her nose from his white chef's jacket, and Paco couldn't miss the look of embarrassment on her face. He had to give her credit, though, for letting the man emote. She waited until he was finished before pulling away.

"I had to stop by to give you my condolences," she said.

Mandrin grabbed the dish towel hanging from his apron and wiped his face. "I have no idea how I'm going to serve lunch, but I have to."

"Why don't you close?"

"Customers will be arriving in fifteen minutes, and over half of the tables are reserved. You know what they say. The show must go on. Come, follow me."

Laure and Paco let Mandrin lead them into the kitchen, gleaming with stainless steel counters and copper pots and pans.

"It's never a good idea to start the service with an empty belly," he said. He sliced into a large loaf of fresh bread. The crust crackled under his knife. He nodded toward a long table. "Get some plates over there and help yourself. Enjoy."

Paco walked over to the table. A commis was setting out platters filled with local specialties. He looked at Laure, knowing she would give names to all the sumptuous-looking dishes arrayed before him.

"This is exactly what I've been talking about," Laure said. She started pointing. "*Jambon persillé*—ham in aspic with tons of green parsley—along with *grattons*, crispy pork cracklings; pistachio and morel sausage; *caillettes,* or pork meatballs with spinach; pressed calf-muzzle salad; *boudin blanc* sausage with foie gras; slices of other local dry sausages; and red-wine-braised *sabodet* sausage."

Paco looked lovingly at each dish, taking a few moments to breathe in the warm spices of the sausage and the crisp scent of the fresh parsley, before pulling out his camera.

"Hey, artist! You're not on the clock. Eat!" Mandrin strode over to hand him a slice of bread with a thick chunk of warm *cervelas* sausage.

Paco didn't need to be asked twice. He bit into it with gusto.

Laure speared a piece of juicy chicken with vinegar and nibbled a few bits of meat. Then she pecked at a custardy chicken liver mousse in an airy crust.

"I see nothing's changed since my article in *Plaisirs de Table,*" she said. "You've mastered the subtle balance of acidity and unctuosity. You're the consummate Lyon chef—excelling in modest, accessible food that's far more complicated to make than it looks."

Mandrin's face got even pinker. Now he was was embarrassed. It was one thing to read a flattering article and another thing altogether to hear such praise from the writer herself.

Paco wolfed down some cured *rosette* and *jésus* sausages with a handful of gherkins before picking up his camera again. The chef allowed Paco to photograph him tasting pepper sauce with a wooden spoon. Then Paco sampled a few small slices of bread garnished with various pâtés that Mandrin insisted he try.

"I made them yesterday," the chef said. "Here's some rabbit pâté, and over there I have a boar pâté. Behind the pâtés I've got a wild mushroom mousse with truffle oil and a balsamic reduction."

Paco looked up briefly and caught Laure staring at the chef, who was eating heartily.

"I can see that Jerome's death hasn't dampened your appetite," she said. Her voice held no judgment, just real astonishment.

Mandrin swallowed his bread, knocked back a full glass of Beaujolais, and wiped his mouth with his sleeve. He looked at Laure with tired eyes. "When you feel as much hunger as grief, then you're still alive."

5

Having said good-bye to Gilles Mandrin, Laure suggested that they get some air with a walk along the Saône River before visiting a few bouchons on the Rue de l'Arbre Sec.

As they neared the quays, Laure zipped her leather jacket, tightened her Hermes scarf, and pulled up her collar to shield her neck. The sky wasn't threatening, and a lovely autumn sun was brushing the tops of the ochre-hued buildings, but the cool breeze felt like it might become a chilly wind.

"I can take some shots of old Lyon," Paco said, digging out an eighty-five-millimeter lens from his bag. He returned the lens a few seconds later without capturing any of the Renaissance pediments or Second Empire façades along the river.

"I thought you wanted to get some photos," Laure said.

Paco gave her a sheepish grin. "You'd think a professional photographer would bring his wide-angle lens. Just don't hold it against me. I'll pick up the lens at the hotel later and come back."

Laure shook her head and smiled. She was an editor and writer, and how many times had she been caught without a pen?

They made their way down the Quai de la Pêcherie, toward the Quai Saint Antoine. The wide sidewalk was lined with plane trees, most of which still had their leaves. Laure was grateful for these few brief moments, when she could take a break from work. She slowed down, focusing on the straight line of trees, and paid no attention to Paco, who was walking at his own pace, keen on framing a perfect image.

Laure passed a city worker, who was picking up discarded papers under cars and benches. Wearing headphones, he was swaying to what she guessed was a Caribbean calypso. A little farther along, a woman with impeccable gray hair was walking a skittish dog. Laure watched as the small Maltese darted over to the side of the walk, sniffed the grass, and squatted. The woman reached into her designer purse, pulled out a small plastic bag, and picked up the droppings. She gave Laure a curt nod and walked away.

When they reached the Quai des Célestins, Laure stopped and turned her attention to the opposite bank, glancing at the Saint Jean and Saint Paul neighborhoods before looking up at the Basilica of Notre-Dame de Fourvière. This sixteenth-century church on the storied praying hill was said to be the center of the city's spiritual and cultural life. It seemed to float in a cloud of greenery.

Laure lingered to take in the view. Then she looked at her watch and turned to find Paco. She spotted him on the Palais de Justice walkway, pointing his camera between the steel tethers. He kneeled in front of the parapet, certainly to calculate the depth of field. An instant later he was leaning over the whirling waters of the Saône, picking up the hazy texture.

Laure watched him for some time, admiring both his talent and his cat-like agility. Then she marched over to join him. "Another change of plans," she said. "Come on."

"Where to now?" he asked.

"You'll know when we get there."

Paco did as he was told, snapping photos as they made their way.

"None of me," Laure ordered.

"But how can my camera ignore your ankles, so straight and well-proportioned in those heels?"

Laure smirked. Corny, yes, but she didn't mind the attention. A second later she heard a bustling behind her. She turned just in time to see two shaggy-haired bike riders careen by Paco, who nearly dropped his camera.

"*¡La puta tu madre!*" he barked.

Laure patted his shoulder and smiled to calm him. His sense of humor was a tad juvenile, but his temper was entirely grown up.

"All in one piece, thank goodness," she said. "We're almost there. It's just a short walk."

6

They arrived at No. 8 Quai Romain Rolland, in front of a stringed instrument shop called Pick & Boch Musique, and Laure rang the intercom. She waited. Finally, the owner of the fifth-floor apartment answered.

"I'll buzz you in," she said.

Laure skipped the elevator and jogged up the stairs, as Paco, weighed down by his equipment and breathing hard, fought to keep up. She arrived on the fifth floor and waited for Paco before knocking. A fortyish woman opened the door and stepped aside to let them in. Her face was wan and tense.

Laure hugged Cecile Frangier, Jerome Thevenay's sister. "I'm so sorry, Cecile," she said. "This is horrible."

Cecile pulled away, wiping her washed-out eyes with a tissue.

Laure turned to Paco. "This is my photographer, Paco. We're in town on assignment."

"Some coffee?" Cecile asked.

"We won't stay. I just wanted to check in to see if you need anything." Laure looked over Cecile's shoulder and noticed two women in the living room. They got up from their chairs and joined them.

"Let me introduce you," Cecile said, putting her arm around Laure's shoulder. "These are my long-time friends Nathalie Chevrion and Veronique Lafarqeau. Veronique is Gilles Mandrin's sister, and Nathalie is Eric Chevrion's sister. The three of us go way back."

"Not as far back as Mother Guy," Veronique winked as she reached out to shake Laure's hand.

"Yes, Mother Guy," Laure said, turning to Paco. "She was the one who served up a red-wine-based eel stew in the mid-eighteenth century to hungry workers on the banks of the Rhône River. Her husband caught the eels. Mother Guy's two granddaughters inherited her restaurant and became well known for the very same recipe."

"That's how it is in Lyon," Veronique said. "The restaurants and recipes are passed from one generation to the next."

"We just ate at your brother's bouchon," Paco said. "The pork meatballs were something else!"

Veronique grinned. "Something else, huh? You haven't tasted mine! I just brought some over to Cecile."

"I can vouch for Veronique's meatballs," Cecile said. "The secret is getting them to bind properly." She turned to her friends. "Thank you so much for thinking of us. The meatballs will go perfectly with your polenta, Nathalie. François will eat well tonight."

"We only wish we could do more," Veronique said. "Call either of us if you need anything."

"But can't you stay for more coffee?" Cecile asked.

"No, we have to get going," Nathalie answered. "We'll see you soon."

With that, the two women left, and Cecile ushered Laure and Paco into her living room. "Stay as long as you'd like. You're no trouble at all. I'll just step into the kitchen and get some coffee for us."

She was gone before Laure could object.

Laure surveyed the apartment. The large living room was flooded with light from the three tall windows overlooking the Saône. The room was modestly furnished but decorated with finesse. Laure admired the hardwood and natural-fiber upholstery. The walls were a pale yellow and a soothing green with white accents. It all felt inviting and comfortable, like the store Cecile and François owned.

"When did you get to town?" Cecile asked, coming back in with a large tray holding three white porcelain cups, a glass French press, and fragrant brioches. "It's been so long since you visited."

"Just this morning," Laure answered, helping her friend set out the cups. "The theme of our January issue is Lyon's bouchons, and we'll be here for a few days. We'd like to do an article on your shop for the Table Art section. I hear you've added a new line of hand-blown Mexican glasses and expanded your terracotta selections. But… Well, we can talk about scheduling an interview later."

"How kind of you to include us. You can make the arrangements with François. I imagine he'll be at the store more than I'll be over the next several days. We were both there when the police called to… Thank God, he was the one who answered the phone. He knew just what to say. He's good at that kind of thing."

"I still can't believe what happened."

Cecile sighed and put her cup down. "I can't either. I still haven't gotten over Mother's death five years ago. We were just at the cemetery, putting flowers on her grave. And now we have to select a new plot."

Laure put her own cup down. "Cecile, do you have any idea of who could have done such a thing? Was Jerome in any kind of trouble?"

"No, not that I'm aware of. At least not recently."

"Has he had any problems in the past?"

"No, not really, although two or three years ago some guy came around to talk to Jerome about purchasing the restaurant, and Jerome didn't like his attitude. He was interested in several bouchons on the Rue Mercière and the Rue Saint Jean. He wanted to turn them into nightclubs. He wasn't from around here, and nobody had seen him before."

"From what I could see, none of the owners agreed to sell," Laure said.

"That's right. Nobody wanted to sell. The guy wasn't expecting that. He had a big budget, and his offers were respectable, but I don't think he understood that bouchons are, well, more than just an ordinary business. Bouchon owners are invested body and soul in what they do."

Laure nodded. "But why do you mention this man? Did he threaten Jerome?"

"No, he didn't do anything, as far as I know, that justified filing a complaint with the police, but I think he didn't expect to have his offers refused. He wasn't used to not getting his way. That's all."

Cecile refilled their cups and continued, "His approach was kind of rough, without being outright threatening. I don't know if I'm being clear. You'll have to excuse me. I'm having a little trouble getting my thoughts straight. We went out to dinner with friends last night, and I had too much to drink. I took something just a couple of hours ago to help me handle the news. Nothing strong, just an herbal remedy, but still..."

"You're being very clear, Cecile. Don't worry. Who doesn't need something under such circumstances?"

"Yes. So, this man seemed to have a way of pressuring people. My brother never said exactly what he was doing, but I could tell he was feeling the heat. Jerome told me the guy liked throwing people in a hot pan and holding the handle."

"I'm guessing Jerome didn't take well to those tactics," Laure said.

"Not at all. He made it clear that the restaurant had been in the family for four generations. He wasn't going to sell."

"Have you given this information to the police?"

"Not yet. In any case, I don't know what they would do with it. The man vanished. Nobody saw him again." Cecile rubbed her temples.

Laure waited a moment. "Cecile, I may be overstepping, but I need to ask you about something: we saw Tony this morning, and he was very distraught. Had Jerome and Tony been arguing?"

"What?" Anger flashed in Cecile's eyes. "Tony loved Jerome, Laure. Of course, he was distraught. My brother was Tony's savior, remember? Maybe the two of them had disagreements from time to time over dishes on the menu or adjustments to the recipes. But arguments? Never!"

"I understand, Cecile. I think the world of Tony…"

Paco cut her short. "But passionate love can sometimes fuel passionate anger."

Laure gave Paco a withering look, shutting him up.

She turned back to Cecile. "I agree with you, Cecile. I'm fond of Tony. But I had to ask."

Laure finished her coffee, gave Paco a nod, and picked up her purse. "We'll leave now so you can rest. I just wanted you to know I'm thinking of you, and we're here if you need anything. We'll call François at the store, as you suggested, and we'll come back to see you again before we leave."

"Thank you," Cecile said. "I do want some peace and quiet right now—and sleep. I have tickets for the opera tonight, and I'll need to rest if I'm going to make it to the show."

"So you're going out?"

"Actually, I'm looking forward to it: *Mozart and Salieri* by Rimsky-Korsakov. They say this opera's very different from his other works, not as exotic and lush, and it has only two singing roles."

Laure frowned. "But are you up to that? Doesn't Salieri murder Mozart in the opera?"

"Yes, he poisons him, in fact. But after what's happened to my brother, I don't mind an operatic death. Unlike my brother, everyone gets to take a final bow."

7

Their schedule would be challenging. Laure had gone over a detailed plan to visit several bouchons but would alter the itinerary if warranted. Work was what it would take to keep her mind off Jerome. The image of her friend sprawled on the floor, his head in a garbage bag and his arms and legs tethered, kept flashing in her mind. She marched down the Rue du Président Édouard Herriot, barely able to contain her anger. Paco had trouble following, harnessed as he was like a pack animal—his ruckpack strapped high, his bag of lenses swinging from his left shoulder, and his tripod case on the right. She heard him breathing hard behind her but didn't slow down.

They explored the bouchons on the Rue de l'Arbre Sec, seeking out the ones that offered hearty servings, fresh ingredients, and a well-balanced wine list. Her criteria included respect for tradition, coupled with a reasonable amount of innovation, friendly atmosphere, and fair prices. Laure understood her expectations were high, but she also knew the residents of Lyon—with hundreds of restaurants to choose from—demanded the same. Those that failed to deliver didn't last long. The food editor looked forward to the discoveries that awaited.

Les P'tits Pères was on Laure's A-list. Here, she tasted the *grillade des mariniers du Rhône*, a slow-cooked beef named for the bargemen who once plied the Rhône River. She also sampled the dessert of the day, *gargouilleau aux poires*, a sweet-smelling pear flan, and took down the recipe.

Paco photographed the modest exterior and the homey dining room, with its checked tablecloths and walls filled with plates, paintings, and knickknacks. Then he captured the chefs in the kitchen.

Laure was sorry she couldn't visit two bouchons she had long admired: Le Potiquet, which had served an outstanding beef filet with morel sauce, and La Poule au Pot, named for one of its house specialties. Both had closed their doors.

Leaving Les P'tits Pères, Laure and Paco headed to old Lyon, across the Pont de la Feuillée. Their goal was to taste Joël Salzi's breaded pig's trotters with mushrooms, herbs, and veal sauce at Les Fines Gueules. They also tried the pork sausage with leeks and shallots and topped with cream.

"Well worth the trip," Laure told Paco as they stepped out on the sidewalk. "If we weren't sampling today, I would have stayed and finished the sausage."

Their final choice was Notre Maison on the Rue Gadagne, run by Bruno Lalleau. Some patrons claimed the establishment's other proprietor was Oggi, the gray striped cat that often sat in the window. This bouchon had won high marks for its beef cheeks and pork roll, slow cooked and served with an accompaniment of potatoes, carrots, and sauce.

Laure now had three reviews—not nearly what she needed, but the other restaurants on their list, although good, weren't worthy of a full article. She'd give them a mention. She also planned to visit restaurants she had panned in the past. If they had gotten better, she would make note of it.

Paco and she had accomplished a fair amount of work, and Laure would have been satisfied if it weren't for the shadow of Jerome's homicide, which seemed to hang over every bouchon in the city. While all the restaurant owners were quick to praise Jerome—who had been likeable, skilled in the kitchen, and a champion of their calling— they hastened to share their anger and concern for their own safety. If it happened to Jerome, could it happen to them? Did they need better locks and cameras, perhaps even security people?

§§§§

Evening enveloped the buildings beneath the Fourvière Hill. Laure and Paco looked away as they passed the shuttered Petit Pouce, sealed off by police tape. They continued until they reached the square providing a direct view of the Basilica of Notre-Dame de Fourvière. Atop the hill, the church glowed in the night, its lights showcasing the stained-glass windows, the portals, and the knights, angels, and mythical animals. To Laure it seemed otherworldly, contrasted as it was against the robust architecture of the buildings bordering the square.

Paco started clicking, zooming in on the statues of the Virgin Mary and the Angel Gabriel and focusing on the details of the stone railings.

"The basilica seems to be inspiring you," Laure said. "We should head up there. You'd have a panoramic view of the city and could get a great shot for a two-page spread in the magazine. What do you think?"

"All the way up there?" he asked.

"Pardon me for suggesting a walk up a hill, although it's not that far."

"May I remind you that I've been carrying three tons of equipment since this morning?"

"In that case, since I pity you and I'm a woman of great compassion, we'll take the *ficelle.*"

Paco finished putting his camera away and looked at her. "We'll take the string?"

"Don't make such a face. It's the funicular. The locals call it the ficelle. The station is nearby."

"That would be better than all those stairs."

"But it won't replace the yoga class I'm missing this week."

The trip took all of two minutes, and they found themselves on the broad esplanade where the nineteenth-century Fourvière basilica reigned, crushing the city with its powerful majesty. Paco trotted off to the portals. This time it was Laure who had to keep up. She watched as he entered the church, signed himself, and raised his eyes to the domed nave. He then slipped a coin into a collection box and lit a candle in the second row of a tall bank of flickering votives wafting the odors of melted wax and burning wicks.

Laure looked away, feeling uncomfortable, even nosy, watching him pray and all but a little lost in the neo-Byzantine sanctuary, built over an ancient Roman forum. The interior was loaded with gilt, marble, stained-glass, and mosaics— all of it meant to convey the Church's power and wealth. This was way too kitsch for her. She stepped outside to wait.

When the photographer emerged, Laure was standing in the shadow of a statue of Pope John Paul II. The pope's arms were open, and his smile was beneficent. He looked ready to fly off to heaven.

"There's a tai chi position that looks a little like that," she said, pointing to the statue.

Paco raised his fingers to his lips to shush her. "No blasphemy, please."

"But I'm not making fun, really."

"I'm becoming acquainted with your sense of humor. I'll just call it unique."

"Acquainted, maybe, but not familiar, let me assure you. And anyway, what would be so scandalous about a pope as energetic and inspired as he was trying out tai chi? Everybody knows it's great for flexibility, strength, and balance."

Paco didn't answer, and Laure turned her attention to the glittering city lying beneath them. They were silent for several minutes. Finally, Paco pulled out his tripod and found his widest lens to capture the view.

Laure pointed and named the sights: "The zinc rooftop is the Theatre des Célestins, and the dome belongs to the Hôtel-Dieu, which used to be a hospital for the needy. It's a museum now. That skyscraper in the Part-Dieu neighborhood is called the Pencil. It's one of the tallest buildings in Europe. The lower floors are offices, and the top floors are a hotel. Those two tall steeples belong to the Saint Nizier Church, and that grandiose roof that looks like an overturned basket is the opera house. Built in the eighteenth century, it was entirely redone at the end of the nineteen eighties by the architect Jean Nouvel." Laure moved her finger to another part of the city. "Over there, you have the baroque classicism of the city hall and the slopes of the Croix Rousse neighborhood."

Paco shot his last photo. "The lights down there look like psychedelic glitter magnified a thousand times over in the inky reflections of the river."

For once, Laure was at a loss for words. Her photographer hadn't needed guidance on framing a photo. Like an accomplished painter, sculptor, or even a true master in the kitchen, Paco had the eye of an artist, which she lacked. That kind of talent was something she admired—without resentment, because she had her own gifts. Laure looked out over the city and let her thoughts wander back to another artist and friend who was no longer.

Paco started packing up his gear. "I'm satisfied," he said. "I think we'll have some splendid photos."

When he turned to look at her, Laure hastily wiped away her tears with her fingertips. leaving a trace of mascara. She pursed her lips to keep them from trembling. "To think some bastard is out there somewhere…"

8

A sharp wind had risen in the Presqu'île, sweeping away the autumn leaves that had fallen since Laure and Paco's arrival. This area, extending from the foot of the Croix Rousse Hill to the confluence of the Rhône and Saône rivers, was the heart of Lyon's shopping, dining, cultural, and government lives. It had been a UNESCO World Heritage Site since 1999, and Laure thought it was the most beautiful part of the city.

Laure and Paco had taken refuge in the bronze-hued warmth of the Café des Jacobins, in front of the area's monumental marble fountain with stone mermaids. The two were sitting in silence, staring at their coffees—long, no sugar for her and double-dose *noisette* with milk for him. The basket of sweet-smelling croissants seemed to tease them, as if they had chosen to be tempted just to offer more resistance.

The evening before, they had dined at the Bouchon des Filles on the Rue du Sergent Glandan, near the Place Sathonay. Although she had heard much about the energetic young owners, this was her first opportunity to make their acquaintance. Isabelle Comerro and Laura Vildi were determined to protect Lyon's culinary traditions, but they weren't afraid to veer into nontraditional territory. Laure would certainly write about this Michelin-starred restaurant, with its glassy soufflé with chartreuse, declination of pralines, and a surprising number of vegetarian options.

Paco had taken countless photos of the interior, paying special attention to the long tables, beamed ceiling, stone-framed doorways, red floral wallpaper, and checked napkins bearing the restaurant's name. The featured dishes of the day were posted on a chalkboard, and a vintage poster celebrated the wines of France. Laure knew that some of Paco's experimental photos, such as those playing with light and shadows, wouldn't be published, but she admired his desire to test what he could do with his camera.

She had watched as Paco packed up his camera and started sampling some dishes: smoked herring, green lentil and cold skate salad, and hanger steak. He had followed up with apple pastry and puddings.

Meanwhile, she had interviewed the owners, learning that they had deep roots in the Lyon bouchon scene and prioritized warmth and friendliness. After winding up the interview, she rejoined Paco and suggested that they polish off the night with a bottle of Morgon.

They had left the restaurant a bit giddy, although not entirely tipsy, and had carefully made their way along the river bank, skirting the Saint Nizier Church to reach the Place des Célestins.

The night had passed too quickly, and their morning ritual, in a café instead of the hotel dining room, was filled with yawning.

As Laure absently stirred her coffee, an elderly man in a knit vest that was too big for his bony shoulders limped over to the counter and climbed onto a stool. He waved to a man who looked similar in age. He had red cheeks and a prominent belly squeezed into a short sweater.

The man with the limp pulled a wadded handkerchief from his pants pocket. He snorted into it twice and wiped his nose. "That's a nasty westerly comin' through."

"Hey, old man Gambil, what can I get you?" the waiter called out.

"A Russian coffee for me."

"What about you, Bambane? The same?"

"A Belgian," said the man with the round belly. From the looks of him, it wasn't his first mug of something stronger than coffee this morning. The waiter poured the ale and opened a bottle of red wine for the Russian "coffee."

"Mandrin kicked the bucket last night," Old Man Gambil said.

"Gilles?"

"That's right, my man. Gilles Mandrin."

"That can't be! What happened?"

Laure and Paco were both wide awake now. They looked at each other, speechless.

The waiter delivered the drinks, and Gambil picked up his cup. "It was on the Rue Mercière. The street cleaners found him. They spotted the back door of his place wide open."

"He was already stiff?" Bambane asked.

"Yep, and more than just a little. He was laid out on the tiles. Poor guy. His head was stuffed in a plastic bag. He got knocked out, most likely, and then they pulled the bag over his head. Looked like he suffocated."

"Did they rob the place, like they did Thevenay's the other night?"

"Yeah. The dude who done it was a pro, for sure. It wasn't a half-assed job."

"Crap. But it's better that way, my friend. Mandrin kicked before he could feel it."

Gambil shook his head. "I wouldn't say that. I hear suffocating's not pretty. But I know one thing for sure. We'll be hearing some wild stories."

"Not my style," Bambane said. "Don't like gossip, but there's one thing I will say: it's just not right, those two guys gettin' done for a handful of bills."

"The whole damned town's gonna go crazy over this. I know some busybodies who're gonna work up a cold sweat."

"Double crap," Bambane muttered into the bottom of his empty mug. He slammed it down and wiped his mouth. "I'm outta here. Had enough to quench my thirst."

"Don't be a wuss. Stay for another."

"No. I'm done talkin'."

"You ain't even got a rainshade. You're gonna take a soakin'."

"Don't care," Bambane said. He heaved himself down from his stool and headed toward the exit, seemingly indifferent to the raindrops that were spotting the sidewalk.

Gambil pushed his cup across the counter. The waiter nodded and started making another drink for him.

Laure felt weak. How long had she been sitting there with her mouth just hanging open? She turned to Paco. "Did you hear what I heard?"

She realized right away there was no need. Paco's dark eyes were filled with worry.

"I'm afraid so," he said.

Laure propped her chin up with her hand to stop the trembling. "Jerome yesterday. Gilles today. It... It..."

"It sucks. It really sucks."

"And to think we were just at his restaurant yesterday, and we met his sister at Cecile's. She must be devastated." Laure leaned back in her chair and took a deep breath, trying to pull herself together. Finally, feeling more confident, she looked at Paco. "I know someone with the local paper, *Le Progrès*, who might be able to give us more information. I'll call him."

"A food writer?"

"No, he's general assignment, although he does cover a lot of political stories. He'll talk to me."

"What's his name?"

"Jean-Philippe Rameau, like the musician."

"Don't know him... What group?"

Laure tilted her head. "What are you talking about?"

"Rameau. What band is he in?"

"Jean-Philippe Rameau was a Baroque composer, knucklehead! Do you do that on purpose?"

"Do what? I told you I didn't know him. No reason to get prickly. So what's your reporter friend like?"

Paco was testing his limits, but she ignored it.

"We met at a ninetieth birthday celebration for Paul Bocuse—you know, the father of nouvelle cuisine. He was named Chef of the Century by the Culinary Institute of America. The event was organized by the Bocuse d'Or Winners. Jean-Philippe was covering it, and we had a nice time."

"Had a nice time?" Paco was studying her face too intently.

Laure didn't answer. She was in no mood to humor her photographer's apparent jealousy. This situation was serious, and he needed to rein it in. She scrolled down her contact list and hit call. Jean-Philippe answered after three rings.

"Hi, Jean-Philippe. It's Laure Grenadier. I'm in Lyon for a few days."

No response. All she could hear was background noise: cars beeping, heels clicking, and a siren somewhere. Where was he?

"Hello? Are you there?" Laure wondered if she had entered the right number. Or had she made a big mistake, thinking he'd be happy to hear from her?

Jean-Philippe Rameau cleared his throat and finally answered. "So, you didn't forget me, after all."

9

Laure felt the heat rising to her cheeks as she set the phone down. She was elated about spending the evening with a talented colleague at one of the best restaurants in Lyon, which had so many excellent options. At the same time, she couldn't ignore the flutters in her stomach. Jean-Philippe wasn't just a fellow writer. They had shared a romantic day after the Bocuse celebration, and since then they hadn't seen each other. Either he was too busy, or she was.

"Good news?" Paco asked.

"You could put it that way. We'll have a long day, but it'll end at La Mère Brazier with Jean-Philippe Rameau."

Laure waved to the waiter, who was behind the counter, shooting the breeze with Gambil and pulling hot cups from the dishwasher. She wanted another coffee.

"That wasn't the plan," Paco protested. "And I don't think it's a good idea. I can't go poking around in the kitchen during the dinner service. They'll kick me out, and with good cause."

"There won't be any problem, Paco, because I'm giving you the night off. I'm going alone. You can go back another day to shoot your photos. Tonight is for something else."

"Something else?"

"Yes, that's right."

Laure reached over to the chair beside her and picked up her purse. She pulled out her tablet and started reviewing their appointments, along with the notes she had made while preparing for the trip. Then she unfolded a map of downtown Lyon to go over the day's plans with Paco. But he seemed preoccupied and distant.

"Are you with me, Paco? I just wanted to give you some context. If you'd prefer that the day be a surprise, I understand."

"No, not at all. It's just... Well, your dinner tonight's no problem."

The waiter appeared before Paco could finish. He banged down the two coffees and removed the dirty cups and empty croissant basket, muttering something about the mess on the table. After he walked away, Laure turned her full attention to Paco, whose sudden pensiveness concerned her.

"You seem anxious," she said, lowering her voice. "Are you still thinking about Gilles?"

"No, that's not what I'm thinking about," Paco mustered a smile. "But I am wondering something."

"And what's that?"

"Well, you said you're going to La Mère Brazier tonight."

"Indeed."

"And we've talked about other restaurants called La Mère, right?"

"Yes."

"So, why do so many bouchons have La Mère in the name? It means mother—why Mother This and Mother That?"

"Of course," Laure said. "I should have explained that already." She sipped her coffee and wiped her mouth with her paper napkin.

"It's thanks to all those mothers that Lyon has bouchons as we know them today. The term Mères Lyonnaises refers to generations of women chefs, beginning with Mother Guy, who made Lyon the undisputed gastronomic capital of France. Many modern-day legends, including Paul Bocuse and Georges Blanc, got their start in the kitchens of these women."

Laure leaned forward, eager to share Lyon's rich and colorful story. She had studied the city's culinary history in earnest and loved talking about it.

"The concept was simple: modest women offering working-class food, plus a few à la carte dishes, in no-frills restaurants. La Mère Fillioux, for example, served a single fixed menu. Their strength lay in raising a few local specialties to the level of perfection—excellence and simplicity combined.

"At first, prices were low and the clientèle mostly local working people. But the phenomenon burgeoned in the second half of the nineteenth century, and it wasn't long before people from all over France were flocking to Lyon's restaurants. Their popularity peaked between the two world wars. You could call that period the golden years.

"What was so golden about it?" Paco asked.

"Several factors were key. There was the development of tourism and food guides. Two or three thousand well-off folks were driving around France at the time, on the lookout for local specialties. The Michelin brothers recognized this new niche and started publishing their guide. Then the economy went into a slump, and many wealthy families had to let their cooks go. So the women who had been working in the kitchens of the wealthy set off on their own—doing what they knew best. By the time World War II broke out, there were thirty of these original bouchons in this region."

"A respectable number," Paco said, looking around. "Should we ask for more croissants?"

Laure frowned. "I think we're fine, Paco. Let me continue. Over time, the clientèle became more well-off, and the menus began to include upscale food, without veering from their origins."

"So tell me about some of the other mothers," Paco said.

"Well, there was Elisa Blanc, who earned a Michelin star in 1929. She won first prize from the Touring Club de France the following year and got her second Michelin star in 1933. The writer Maurice Edmond Sailland—known to most as Curnonsky—called her the world's best cook."

"She was Georges Blanc's grandmother, right? And wasn't Curnonsky the guy who called Lyon the gastronomic capital of the world?"

"Correct on both counts, Paco. Then there was Marie Bourgeois. She earned three Michelin stars from 1933 to 1937. She also won the Paris Culinary Prize in 1927. And of course, we can't forget Eugénie Brazier."

"I've heard of her," Paco said. "Actually, she's pretty famous."

"Both famous and accomplished," Laure said. "She was the first woman to earn three Michelin stars and the first French chef to win six in all. Eugénie ran two restaurants, one on the Rue Royale, and another in the Alpine foothills. Her cooking attracted politicians and celebrities including Charles de Gaulle, Valery Giscard d'Estaing, and Marlene Dietrich. The actress loved Eugénie's sweet lobster drenched in cream and brandy.

"And it wasn't just politicians and celebrities who ate at Lyon's salt-of-the-earth bouchons. The

Empress Eugénie dined at the restaurant run by Mere Guy's granddaughters. And Agha Khan often ate at La Mère Bourgeois."

Laure paused and looked out the café window. "There's one woman, though, whose story appeals to me especially. It's Clotilde Bizolon's. Clotilde lost both her husband and her son, Georges, during World War I. When Georges died, she kept a promise she had made to him. She would support France's young fighting men, no matter what.

"She put together a plank-and-barrel stand at the Perrache train station and passed out free lunches, coffee, and wine, along with words of encouragement. News of her work spread, and with the help of an American benefactor, she built a rough shack outside the station, where she could do even more.

"Clotilde turned her deceased husband's shoemaking shop into a restaurant after the armistice and continued her charitable work. She was decorated with the Legion of Honor. And when war broke out again, she opened another refreshment stand at the train station, where, as she had earlier, she passed out free lunches.

"I'd like to tell you Clotilde died peacefully in her sleep after a long life, but I can't. She was assaulted in her home in 1940 and died of her injuries a few days later. Although there was an arrest, there was never a conviction, and the case has gone unsolved."

Laure couldn't even imagine losing a child. And then picking up and doing such heroic work? Unbelievable. She took a last sip of her coffee. It was cold and had lost its fruity aroma.

"I know I'm going on and on, but I do need to tell you about Le Mère Lea Bidault. We'll see her restaurant, La Voûte Chez Lea, this afternoon. She earned a Michelin star for her Champagne sauerkraut. 'Cooking and making love are the same,' she said. 'They both stem from the desire to give pleasure.' But it's her spunk, not her love of feeding people, that I like best. The cart she pushed at the market had a sign. It read: 'Warning! Little woman with big mouth!'

"I just love these women, Paco. They had big hearts, big mouths, and big ambitions, regardless of their size. And they accomplished so much with so little. It's an inspiration."

Paco grinned. "I know women like that. They're my mother, sisters, and grandmothers. Maybe they don't own restaurants, but they make their presence known. And, man, can they cook."

"I don't doubt that you came from a family of fine women, Paco. Look at how you turned out."

"So you think I'm okay, huh?"

Laure gave him an annoyed look. "Don't let it go to your head." She glanced at her watch and decided it was time to wrap up her story. "Of course, things are different today. Practically all of Lyon's bouchons are run by men. And Nouvelle

Cuisine came about in the 1970s. It was another philosophy. But these women were the foundation of Lyon's culinary traditions. Do you know who apprenticed with Eugénie Brazier?"

"Yes, I know: Paul Bocuse."

"Right. Bocuse. The Cook of the Century got his start with La Mère Brazier. The great man would perhaps be nothing, were it not for this good woman—who, by the way, was also a tough boss. He told America's Anthony Bourdain, 'She was such a screamer, you would fall on your ass, she was screaming so hard.' How would you have liked working for her?"

"No, thank you."

Laure paid their tab and collected her things. She was wide awake now and ready to start the day. Her talk with Paco had allowed her to temporarily forget about the murders. But they were still there, lingering in her consciousness.

10

Laure Grenadier and Paco Alvarez spent the day visiting one bouchon after another. Every restaurant welcomed them warmly, mostly because of Laure's reputation for integrity. Some had suffered less-than-glowing reviews in *Plaisirs de Table*, but they didn't appear to hold it against her. They seemed to appreciate their conversations with the editor-writer, perhaps realizing that her comments were warranted. For her part, Laure was eager to help the restaurants improve. She avoided hurtful and peremptory remarks and tried her best to be fair in her assessments of the menus, dishes, atmosphere, and décor, even to the point of suggesting changes.

As the day went on, the tastings multiplied: artichoke foie gras, Richelieu pâté, calf's head with *ravigote* sauce, crayfish quenelles, white-wine-glazed mackerel, lentil and *cervelas* salad, chicken-liver cakes, Saint Marcellin cheese, and *cervelles de canut*. None of the specialties were neglected.

Meanwhile, Paco prowled the rooms, looking for the details embodying the essence of each business: a sign with two clover-chewing pigs, highly polished wooden benches, reproductions of a Guignol theater, sepia lithographs, old enameled plaques, tin candlesticks and colored glass bobbles, beveled tiles from another age, napkins folded into white-cotton bouquets, and reflections on gleaming pots.

Certain subjects came up time and again: slow business, the difficulty of finding qualified staff, and, inevitably, the two deaths that had bloodied the reputation of the bouchons in under forty-eight hours. No one had an explanation for the homicides, not even a theory, but the tension was palpable. Laure sensed that the chefs and owners needed to talk about the murders, if only to relieve their anxieties.

They stopped work to avoid disturbing the noon service and decided to have lunch at the Bistrot de Lyon. Laure contented herself with a green salad embellished with bacon, croutons, and a poached egg, as she wanted to save her appetite for the afternoon tastings. Paco took in the black and white tiles, the paintings, and the dark woodwork before ordering the rolled veal head with *gribiche* sauce.

As she pecked at her salad, Laure tried to read the customers' faces. Most of them looked preoccupied or on edge. From time to time, she caught snatches of frightened conversation. The homicides seemed to be on everyone's mind, and the cozy atmosphere of the bouchon wasn't reassuring them in the least.

Paco, however, seemed oblivious to the agitation. When his plate arrived, Laure watched with amusement as he studied and sniffed it. He slowly raised his fork to his mouth. And then his face lit up with surprise and delight.

Laure almost laughed. "The cold-egg sauce is delicious, isn't it?" she said as Paco dug in.

The afternoon proceeded according to plan. Laure sampled the specialties and made copious notes while Paco took hundreds of photos.

Night was falling when they returned to the hotel, relieved to have stuck to their schedule. Many of the places they had visited—Le Vivarais, Chez Mounier, Le Poêlon d'Or, La Voûte Chez Léa, Chez Sylvie, and La Mère Jean—had met—and even exceeded—their expectations. Although the homicides were eating at everyone, the food in the city's bouchons hadn't suffered.

11

Finally in her room, Laure fell on her bed with delight, threw her leather boots on the carpet, and unfastened the top button of her jeans. She was tired, but she still had to get dressed for the evening and call Daphne Fromentin, her editorial assistant at the magazine.

After closing her eyes for a few minutes, she got up and summoned two thousand years of Indian wisdom to re-energize. She put her feet together and assumed Tadasana, the starting pose. She took a deep breath and raised her arms above her head, tightening her leg muscles to avoid arching her back. She relaxed her neck and created space between each vertebra.

Then she leaned forward and placed her hands on the floor to relieve the tension in her pelvis and lower back. Uttanâsana was an intense stretch that brought calm and peace of mind. After a few minutes of exercise, Laure was ready to call the office.

"Hi, Daphne." Laure examined the fruit pastes on her bedside table and picked one up as she waited for a response. "Daphne, are you there?"

Finally, an answer: "Sorry, Laure. Yes, I'm here. Have you gotten through all your assignments for the day?"

"Yes, mission accomplished. Now I can take care of... Everything else! But I can tell something's wrong. What is it?"

Daphne groaned. "If only it were one thing. Actually, we've got our hands full back here."

Laure put the fruit paste down. "Okay, what's going on?"

"First, there's a huge problem with this month's feature on scallops. The photos of the sautéed scallops with parsley and the citrus scallop carpaccio are a disaster. We can't use any of them."

"That's bad. A hell of a lot of preparation went into shooting the carpaccio. Now we've got to start again from scratch."

"We also have a big problem with the photos for the Fresh From the Market section."

"How big?" Laure felt the tension slipping into her shoulders again.

"You can't tell the difference between the shrimp that are fresh out of the water, all glossy and translucent, and the ones that are covered with black spots and spoiled."

The Fresh From the Market feature had been Laure's baby years earlier, when she was hired. The idea was helping readers make smart purchases by showing four or five photographs of meat or produce going from fresh to a state of decomposition over several days.

The news was upsetting, but Laure took care to stay calm. The last person she wanted to vent on was Daphne, one of the most capable and hard-working staff members at the magazine.

"You understand, Laure. We can't use the photos, and we don't have any backups. We might have to scrap the whole section this month." Daphne fell silent for a moment. "There is one possible solution—if you could spare Paco. He's our most efficient and reliable photographer."

"Uh-uh. He's too busy here. But we still have some time before we go to press, so we should be able to pull everything together. We've faced more challenging issues in the past."

"I haven't told you about the freelancer who was doing the interview with the scuba-diving fisherman. He's fallen off the radar. And the other freelancer handling the shopping section has missed his deadline. I might have to dig up other writers for those features. And now we have additional ads, which is both good and bad. Good because it means more money and bad because they've bumped up our pages."

"Oh no!" Laure's composure fell away. She took a deep breath. "Okay," she whispered. "It's not a pretty picture, but things could be worse. Our computers haven't gone down, have they?"

"Uh, no. Not yet."

Laure went silent, the phone against her ear as she searched for a way to add hours to the day. A few minutes later, she had a plan. "Daphne?"

"Yes."

"I'll ask Paco to go ahead and take his photos at Bocuse tomorrow. I'll do my interviews later. I'll catch the seven or seven-thirty TGV to Paris and should be in the office no later than ten-thirty."

"That works! Enjoy your evening, and see you tomorrow."

Laure hung up and let out a string of swear words, something she'd never do in front of Daphne or any other member of her team. She briefly considered canceling her dinner with Jean-Philippe at La Mère Brazier and calling it a night but changed her mind. She'd keep her date, but only after a hot and fragrant bath to forget her accumulated stress and fatigue, Gilles Mandrin's smile, Cecile Frangier teary eyes, and the heavy atmosphere that prevailed in the city's restaurants.

As soon as the tub was filled with bergamot- and jasmine-scented bubbles, Laure slipped her toes in. From foot to neck, a shiver ran through her body—a good omen for the rest of the evening.

12

Laure left nothing to chance. Her little black dress nipped her perfectly at the waist, highlighting her narrow hips. The slash neck revealed just enough, and the three-quarter sleeves accentuated the delicacy of her wrists. For jewelry, she wore only red carmine earrings that matched her silk clutch. To further lengthen her figure, she had selected eleven-centimeter heels. Although they wouldn't allow for any romantic walks, they could serve as inducement for an intimate taxi ride back to her hotel—provided Jean-Philippe had earned it.

Jean-Philippe. The man blew hot and cold, no doubt about it. Most of the men in her life, including her ex-husband, Nathan, had pursued her, making their amorous intentions known at the very outset and not letting up. But none of those relationships had worked out. The men had been either too cloying or too controlling. And she wasn't a woman who could be controlled or swayed by excessive sentiment.

Maybe a man like Jean-Philippe was better—someone who wouldn't try to run her life, someone who was as dedicated to his work as she was to hers. They did have that shared passion—writing—and it intrigued her. And then there was the day they had spent together. Jean-Philippe had been nothing but attentive, affectionate, and funny. He had made love to her tenderly, satisfying her completely, and afterward they had talked for hours, still naked in bed. But she hadn't seen him since. What was it with him? She intended to find out.

Riding to the restaurant, Laure contemplated the flickering lights on the Quai Jean Moulin. To the right, the Rhône River flowed without tumult, almost well-behaved enough to make residents forget past floods.

Laure loved this city, so full of history. Her magazine's bouchon issue would most certainly give special attention to the legendary Eugénie Brazier, whose story was as engrossing as her food. After losing her mother at the age of ten, she was sent to work on a farm. Nine years later, when she found herself pregnant and unmarried, her father locked her out of the house. She moved to Lyon with her young son, working first for a bourgeois family that had made its fortune in pasta and then for Françoise Fillioux.

According to Eugénie, Françoise was a harsh and jealous woman. She was nearly fired for making a rabbit dish that Françoise often prepared for the staff meal. Eugénie's boss had flown into a rage when she learned the workers preferred Eugénie's rabbit. Later, when customers raved over Eugénie's roasted chicken, Françoise claimed that she was just a dishwasher.

Eventually, Eugénie saved enough money to open a small restaurant in a vacant grocery store, where she prepared dishes including pigeon with peas, crayfish in mayonnaise, and apple flambee—a favorite of her son, Gaston. Her stove provided the restaurant's only heat, and she had to borrow her chairs. A nearby baker finally had forty chairs delivered to the restaurant, saying it wasn't right to make her customers stand while they were eating.

Over time, the restaurant grew and became well appointed. The silver gleamed. The crystal sparkled, and the linen was starched and pressed. Eugénie, known for her fastidiousness, inspected everything. She had the refrigerators emptied and cleaned every day. She later recalled in a cookbook that a poultry supplier had grumbled he would soon be forced to manicure his chickens before delivery.

This account always made Laure chuckle. In her feature, she would highlight the 1945 arrival of Mère Brazier's most famous apprentice: Paul

Bocuse, a wounded and decorated soldier home from the war. Eugénie put Bocuse through his paces at her second restaurant in Col de la Luere, where he not only learned how to cook, but also cared for the vegetable garden, milked the cows, and did the laundry and ironing. With Eugénie Brazier, he mastered the art of turning out pure and simple meals.

The taxi left the quays, turned right, and headed toward the Rue Royale. As they approached No. 12, Laure recognized the red-and-white La Mère Brazier sign and the iron grates, both austere and delicate, over the windows.

The maître d'hôtel rushed over as soon as he spotted her. "Madame Grenadier, what a pleasure to see you. I'm so terribly sorry. Monsieur Rameau called for a reservation today, and every one of our private rooms has been booked for months. All I have left is a table near the counter."

Laure gave him a gracious smile. "I'm sure a very pleasant evening awaits us."

Jean-Philippe was waiting, elbows on the table and entirely focused on his smartphone, as if he had been there for some time already. He seemed oblivious to the room's refined and harmonious blend of wood and faience, beige and blue-gray tones, and crystal, linen, and china.

Laure told the maître d'hôtel that she could make her own way to the table. She slipped into her chair, unacknowledged. Finally, Jean-Philippe detached himself from his screen, looking confused and hesitant, as if the choice between standing up to greet her with a kiss and reading the last part of the text weren't obvious.

Laure shot him a cool look. "I assume you'll let me know when you can join me."

He slipped his phone into a pocket and looked straight at her with a broad smile. "Laure! How good it is to see you, and at such a historic restaurant."

Amused by his attempt to recover from his blunder, Laure allowed him to get bogged down in a string of platitudes before finally participating in the conversation. It meandered from the nearby Rue Eugénie Brazier, the street renamed in 2003, to Mathieu Viannay's tenure as manager. He had taken over the restaurant in 2008 and had earned it two Michelin stars. Laure and Jean-Philippe also admired the Art Deco tiles, the floor, and the famous windows.

"You know, I couldn't have gotten a table tonight if I hadn't dropped your name," he whispered. "I did, and then 'open sesame,' here we are."

Laure smiled coyly. "So, Jean-Philippe, have you read *One Thousand and One Nights*?"

"Indeed, I have." He paused, taking in her auburn hair, which she had styled in loose waves, and simple carmine earrings. "Perhaps we'll have the opportunity to read it to each other one day. Or maybe you could just tell me stories, like

Sheherazade. I treasure some memorable stories from the day we spent together."

He gave her a soft smile, and Laure felt herself starting to blush. She picked up her menu and began reading, hoping her cheeks would go back to their natural color. "I'd love the *poulette de Bresse en vessie*," she finally said, glancing up. "Encasing the chicken in a pig's bladder takes poaching to an entirely different level. It's for two, though."

"I had my eye on the *pain de brochet croustillant aux écrevisses*, with the spring vegetables and lobster sauce. But for you, Laure, I will share the chicken—as long as you promise to come back with me before your stay is up."

Laure pretended to think about it. "I might be able to squeeze some time into my schedule."

The sommelier had Laure taste a Morey-Saint Denis premier cru, a Les Ruchots vintage from Domaine Amiot. It was a racy, elegant, and powerful wine, which she took the time to chew and enjoy as the tannins melted. She nodded her approval.

Jean-Philippe raised his glass. "To friendship. May ours be bright, supple, and just a bit racy."

Laure almost winced. Too many wine allusions spoiled a good toast—and could easily break the spell. She went neutral. "To life."

"You're right," Jean-Philippe said as the crystal glass met his lips. "I've been appreciating it even more these days, considering what's going on around here."

Laure nodded and put her glass down. "So true. Did you know the chefs?"

"I wouldn't say we were close, but I was friendly with both of them, especially Gilles Mandrin."

Two waiters approached and waited to be noticed before announcing the *mises en bouche*. With reverential silence, Laure and Jean-Philippe tasted their appetizers. Laure closed her eyes to concentrate on the flavors.

Jean-Philippe didn't follow suit. "And you?" he said, yanking Laure out of her state of beatitude. "I suppose you knew their work well."

"Yes, I've stayed in touch with them over the years. Do you know if the police have any leads?"

Jean-Philippe lifted his glass again and sniffed the wine before responding. "Let's just say they have no suspects. But..."

He glanced around the room, and Laure did the same. The other diners didn't appear to be paying them any mind. They were conversing in hushed voices and seemed to be absorbed in their food.

"What exactly do you know?" he asked.

"I understand Jerome and Gilles were beaten and smothered in sacks, and the night's take was stolen. That's all."

"Well, keep what I'm about to tell you to yourself. The police aren't talking about it, as they don't want to give away any clues or spread panic. Thevenay and Mandrin were murdered exactly the same way. Someone hit them in the back of the head and bound their hands and feet. Then, while they were blacked out, he stuffed their heads in the garbage bags, knotted rope around their necks, and had them suffocate."

"What a horrible way to go. So there's no doubt that the two homicides were identical?"

"In every detail. The police think the same man committed both homicides."

"When you say the same man, what are you implying?"

"It may well be a serial killer who's targeting Lyon's bouchon owners."

Laure gulped her burgundy, as if it could help her absorb what she had just learned. A waiter immediately filled their glasses and whisked away the empty verrines.

"But why? For a few euros?"

"It's true that the night's take was stolen, but the investigators don't think robbery was the motive. A robber wouldn't have gone to such extremes. He would have slipped in, done his dirty work, and gotten out. Obviously, this is more complex."

Laure weighed what Jean-Philippe had just told her. "You're saying it's some kind of ritual, a signature, some sort of revenge, perhaps?"

Jean-Philippe's eyes brightened as he looked at her. He had an affectionate smile on his lips.

"I can tell by your expression that you think I watch too many crime shows on TV," Laure said. "Ritual slayings, signatures, revenge..."

"Not at all. You're on the money, but our problem is that the signature is the only clue the police have. There was nothing at the sites: no fingerprints, no traces left behind that could betray the murderer. *Nada.* Forget DNA—you can imagine the difficulty of investigating a crime committed in a crowded place like a restaurant."

"They have no idea what the killer used to knock out the two men?"

Jean-Philippe shook his head. "Plus, there weren't any witnesses."

"Well," said Laure, "I actually have some information to share with you."

Without mentioning her source, Laure related the story of the mysterious stranger intent on buying Lyon's bouchons and turning them into nightclubs.

"I heard that story a few years ago, but I don't believe it," Jean-Philippe said.

"Why?"

"Because everybody knows that bouchons live on after the death of their owners. They're passed down or purchased. Murder is not the way to go about a takeover in a town like this."

"But maybe the point isn't just killing the owners. Maybe he wants to intimidate the owners of the other restaurants and spread fear."

"Well, if that's what he's trying to do, the police are interfering with his plans, because very few people know that the two chefs were murdered the very same way."

"In any case, you seem quite familiar with the investigation. Are you covering it for *Le Progrès*?

"I am," Jean-Philippe confirmed, turning his attention to the two waiters who had approached the table with their chicken dish. The waiters presented it with relish, making sure Laure and Jean-Philippe noted the thin slices of truffle atop the bladder.

Laure shivered when she realized the metaphor: like the chefs, the finely prepared chicken she was about to eat had been trussed and stuffed in a bag. But she tried to let it pass. How many times in her life would she be dining on this very dish in this very place?

With a clear and precise gesture, one waiter cut off the chicken breast and arranged the slices on plates that the second waiter had garnished with vegetables. After dismembering the entire bird, the waiters returned the thighs and wings to the kitchen, where they would be kept warm for the second course.

When they were alone again, Jean-Philippe resumed. "I think the case will be taking up a good part of my time. My editor has asked me to stay on it."

"Do you really think the investigation will be long and complicated?" Although Laure was appreciating the delicate aroma of the broth the chicken had been simmered in for hours, she couldn't quite shake the image of the trussed chefs.

"I have a hunch that it's just beginning."

"What are you suggesting?"

"We're talking about a serial killer—remember? The first murder was two nights ago, at the end of the service. The second murder occurred last night, same time. Who says it will stop there? Maybe in two to three hours, in another bouchon, another unsuspecting chef counting his receipts will wind up smothered, his head in a garbage bag."

"You think our killer could strike again tonight?"

"Seems logical to me. That's why I was reading my text messages when you arrived. I've asked my contacts around town to keep an eye out—to text me right away if they see any odd-looking strangers hanging around the restaurants, or some clue turns up. I've got to stay on top of things."

"Of course."

"Now, enough of this murder and mayhem." Jean-Philippe picked up a bite-sized piece of poultry with his fork and passed it to Laure. "Shall we taste?"

13

When Laure returned to the hotel, she found Paco alone in the small sitting room that adjoined the reception area. He was hunched over the coffee table, flicking pistachios between an empty beer bottle and an empty glass. She couldn't help but notice there were more deflected shots than goals. The photographer had taken over three of the room's four beige chairs. The plastic wrapper of a convenience-store sandwich was lying on the chair to his right, and his laptop was on the chair to his left. Laure figured he had been going through the day's photos, cropping and retouching as needed.

Despite his strategic view of the reception area, Paco didn't appear to notice her until he fell back in his chair and stretched his arms above his head.

"You're back." He sounded surprised. "Alone... So soon?"

"Soon? It's not all that early. I see you're still up."

"I was working."

"I can tell," she said, glancing at the pile of pistachio shells on the table. She picked up the empty glass and sniffed it.

"I'm guessing you didn't do any yoga, as I suggested," she said, plopping into the armchair across from him.

"I'm not like you—into yoga and all kinds of martial arts. I prefer cardio. Soccer's my sport." He took the glass from her and started gathering up the shells.

"Did you have a nice evening?"

"The meal was delicious. La Mère Brazier certainly deserves its two stars. Mathieu Viannay came out to talk to us when we were done. I wish we could have stayed longer. I wanted to ask him about the scallop mousse he uses with his quenelles. He refused to put them on his menu until he perfected that lighter mousse. But I've got to be up early, and the very thought makes me tired."

Paco had risen from his chair to collect the pistachio shells strewn on the thick brown carpet.

"I'm making a quick trip to Paris," Laure told him, noticing what looked like relief on his face. "Daphne needs my help. We have to reshoot some photos, chase down two freelancers, and fill extra pages we weren't expecting."

"Do you want me to handle the Bocuse shoot on my own tomorrow?"

"That would be great. Anyway, Paco, Jean-Philippe's been put on the murders. He thinks they might be the work of a serial killer who could strike again. It gives me the chills. Here we are, chatting quietly, and maybe somebody is being murdered somewhere—perhaps even one of the chefs we talked to today."

"That's crazy. Did you ask him about Tony or tell him about the strange man Cecile mentioned?

"To answer your first question—no, I didn't mention Tony because it's nonsense. As for the second question, he had already heard the story, and he doesn't think it's related. In any event, he didn't dwell on it."

"And what about the money that was stolen?"

"The night's take disappeared, but, like the police, he's convinced robbery wasn't the motive."

Laura heard a ping. She picked up her clutch and pulled out her phone to read the message.

"Are you waiting for someone?" Paco asked.

Once again, Laure noted the impertinence. She was fond of her No. 1 photographer, but his fondness for her was beginning to wear thin. She would have to address it. Not now, though. She had more pressing things on her mind. She'd do it at the right time and in the right way—not only because she wanted to keep Paco on her staff, but also because she didn't want to hurt him.

She looked up from her phone. "No Paco, I wasn't waiting for anyone. But when you're the parent of an adolescent girl, and you're away from home for an extended time, you check your messages at all hours of the day and night, especially the night."

Laure unlocked the screen and felt a wave of relief. "Well, it's not Amandine."

"It must be Rameau. I bet he doesn't want you to go to Paris."

"No, it's Cecile. The funeral is the day after tomorrow, eleven o'clock."

"Are you going?"

"Of course. I don't know what we're supposed to be doing at that time, but we'll manage. Well, I'm off to bed. I have to be up in..."

She grabbed Paco's wrist and looked at his watch. "I'd rather not do the math," she said, sighing. "Good night."

"Good night, Laure. Try not to think too much about those murders. They've already ruined your hot date with Rameau."

Laure looked back at Paco. "Ruined? I wouldn't say that."

"Oh?" Paco said, raising an eyebrow.

"Some meals whet the appetite," she said. "Other meals satisfy the appetite."

Paco didn't need to know the intimate details or the lack of them. Laure waved goodnight and watched as he tossed a pistachio in the air and caught it in his mouth.

14

Just off the train, Laure Grenadier jumped into a taxi and headed to her magazine's offices on the Rue du Montparnasse, where staff members had been on deck since seven that morning. She reviewed what needed to be done, including how they could fill the extra pages. By the time she reached the top floor of the building, she had concluded that the task was daunting but not impossible, so long as they didn't get bogged down.

She felt the tense energy as soon as she walked through the door. A proofreader was yelling at one of the interns while two graphic artists stared at their computer screens, clearly pretending they weren't hearing anything.

"I need those pages now!" the proofreader shouted. "How long can it take you to walk across the room?"

Another person Laure needed to talk to. The proofreader had no business dumping on a kid that way. She added it to her to-do list.

Laure was relieved to see that the two freelancers had shown up to complete their articles.
Daphne was looking over the shoulder of one of
the writers. "The copy desk needs that piece in
twenty minutes," she said. "They'll kill me if it's
not there, and I'm indispensable at the moment.
So finish up."

Daphne's early morning e-mail had outlined
the problems, including another one that had
popped up. The columnist handling the In Your
Kitchen section was balking at a request to tweak
a rude response to a sixty-year-old reader's question. There was no reason to alienate people when
magazine subscriptions were dipping. But the columnist wasn't listening to Daphne. Laure would
have to step in and charm the writer into redoing
a few lines.

Laure, mustering a smile, motioned to Daphne,
who walked over to join her. "Have we found a
photographer to fix the scallop debacle?" she asked.

"In theory, yes. I'll know for sure by noon,"
Daphne answered, adjusting the braided leather
and metal necklace that accentuated her generous cleavage.

"I think we'll have enough copy that we didn't
use in our earlier issues to fill the extra space. If not,
we can run more letters from our readers and use
the kids' cooking feature we've been saving for the
next issue. That should do it."

"Sounds good. The copy desk and layout people have been here for hours already. They're cranking out the pages."

"I can see," Laure said, looking around the open-concept offices. Warm autumn light was coming through the windows now and bathing the floor in a soft gold. "Thanks, Daphne. "I don't know what I'd do without you."

Daphne had been working at the magazine for more than five years. When she applied for her position as editorial assistant, Laure had seen past the two piercings in her left nostril, the spiked raven-color hair, eyes heavily lined in black, and patchouli scent.

She could tell right away that Daphne had the chops, and she hadn't been proved wrong. This assistant was smart, efficient, and talented.

The two walked back to Daphne's desk to go over what still needed to be done, and before she had even taken her seat, Laure spotted the fresh croissant wrapped in a paper towel next to the computer.

"Have you given up on your diet?"

"Not at all. I've just started a new one. The last eating plan wasn't doing it for me anymore."

"What was it again?"

"The Chromatic Diet," Daphne said. "It's from a novel. You eat nothing but red foods one day, green foods another day, yellow foods the next— that sort of thing."

Laure raised an eyebrow. "I guess it's creative, if nothing else."

"Yes, that it is. And it takes a lot of work to come up with a meal plan for each day. For example, dairy-free winter-squash soup, a small piece of cheese, and cantaloupe for dessert on orange day; tomato sauce over red-lentil pasta for red day; and spinach salad and roasted vegetables for green day. Conceptually, you just can't eat as much, because the diet demands too much planning. Plus, it's too rigid. It would have made for a great editorial spread—think of the visuals—but the science wasn't there."

"Right. The photos would have been terrific," Laure said, staring at the croissant. "So, what about that little buttery baked item? Is the science for that there?"

"It's my breakfast! I decided to go with a very old concept." Daphne opened a desk drawer and pulled out Ali-Bab's *Encyclopedia of Practical Gastronomy.*

"You're telling me that to slim down, you're following the advice of a man who weighed a hundred and fifty kilos and suggested meals consisting of at least three courses, in addition to appetizers, vegetables, cheeses, fruits, and desserts?"

"He managed to lose forty kilos in eight months, so it must work."

Skeptical, Laure picked up the book and started leafing through the 1,213 pages of the 1907 food bible, which contained thousands of recipes and wise advice on how to cook and host. A metro ticket was tucked in the chapter entitled "Treatment of Obesity for Gourmands." She took a look.

Breakfast
250 grams of sugar-free tea and a small croissant

Lunch
200 grams of any meat, prepared in any way
300 grams of blanched green vegetables sautéed in butter or sprinkled with melted butter
Salad
250 grams of fruit, raw or cooked without sugar

Around two o'clock in the afternoon
A cup or two of chamomile or linden tea, and, if necessary, a glass of water or lemonade at five o'clock

Dinner
Two eggs prepared any way, or a chicken limb, or a small fish, or, during hunting season, small game: thrush, quail, two larks, half a partridge, etc.
200 grams of green vegetables sautéed in butter, or a salad
250 grams of fruit, raw or cooked without sugar

In the evening
A cup or two of tea or an infusion of some sort, a
grog, and, at bedtime, a glass of water

No more than 100 grams of butter per day in all

"I'm surprised, but I guess it makes sense," Laure said. "Veggies and protein, although I'd advise a little less butter." She closed the book and examined the pastel-hued cover. "You know what? We should think about a new section."

"Not on the diets, I hope."

"No, we're not a health and fitness magazine. We're about the pleasure of eating fine food and the skill that goes into creating it. I was thinking about a section dealing with the greats of culinary history—Auguste Escoffier, Marie-Antonin Carême, François Pierre de la Varenne, Jean Anthelme Brillat-Savarin, and others. But we wouldn't handle them in an ordinary way. We'd look at one specific accomplishment that each person made and tell it like a story. For example, how did Marie-Antonin Carême's friendship with Charles Maurice Talleyrand, the diplomat, lead to the invention of the piping bag in the early nineteenth century? What do you think?"

"I like it! Carême and his piping bag would make a great story, but maybe we could start with Ali-Bab. We have so much of his narrative to choose from."

"Right about that," Laure said. "Our Henri Babinski led quite a life. A Polish mining engineer who traveled the world—in search of gold in Brazil, French Guyana, and the United States—before becoming a gourmand, food authority, and writer. It was the primitive chow in the mining camps that motivated him to explore the exotic culinary offerings of the countries where he was living."

"An example of turning an obstacle into an opportunity." Daphne said.

"His credo was, 'If it is indecent to live for eating, it is suitable, while eating to live, to try to fulfil this task, as all others, the best you can and with pleasure.'" Laure quoted from memory. She was feeling inspired.

"I wasn't aware that you were so familiar with his book," Daphne said. "You wouldn't exactly call it a best seller, although I shouldn't be surprised. You're a walking food encyclopedia."

Laure smiled. "I do remember a few things from all the time I spent at Le Cordon Bleu and the Sorbonne. But as for Henri Babinski, he still has his admirers. "He was a pioneer, after all."

"Tell me, how did he come by his nom de plume?"

"Apparently, he chose Ali-Bab because *alis* or *alius* means 'other' in Latin, and Bab is a diminutive of Babinski. He considered himself the 'other Babinski,' as his brother Joseph was a famous neurologist. But *baba* also means 'cake' in Polish. So who knows."

Daphne's phone rang. She glanced at her screen. "It's the photographer. I've got to take this."

Laure checked her own texts. There was nothing new since her daughter's last message. As she had suspected, Amandine wouldn't be getting together with her after school. She had a "thing with her girlfriends." Amandine, so bright and affectionate when she was little, had recently become distant, even a touch disrespectful. Laure resolved to see what was going on with her daughter when she finished her work in Lyon.

Paco hadn't sent anything. Lyon was probably calm, and Jean-Philippe's predictions hadn't played out. The murders had stopped. Unless...

Laure wasn't a patient person by nature. She hated uncertainty and took charge whenever she needed to. In doubt, she sent a text.

15

The taxi dropped off Paco near the Auberge du Pont de Collonges, and he knew right away that he was about to enter a destination sought out by food lovers everywhere. The building, with stone walls at the pedestrian level and Paul Bocuse's family home—green with red shutters—above it, rose imposingly over the Saône River, the triumphant lighthouse of French gastronomy. If there was any doubt, a large sign atop the building announced the chef's name, and his image presided over the parking lot. Nothing was left to chance here, from the smallest doorknob to the polished cobblestones, from the flower boxes to the festoons on the roof. Paco had reached the most prestigious table in the universe.

He stepped up to the courtyard, where a trompe-l'œil fresco, in the spirit of those that had brightened Lyon's buildings since the nineteen seventies, dominated a wall. Some forty meters long, the mural was called the Rue des Grands Chefs.

It paid tribute to those who had made culinary history. Bocuse had wanted to capture the legendary chefs for eternity, to represent them life-sized at their stoves and work tables. The hyperrealism of the dishes in front of them made Paco salivate.

There was Carême, Escoffier, Alexandre Dumaine, and Fernand and Marie-Louise Point. He recognized Eugénie Brazier and Mother Fillioux, under the eye of Édouard Herriot, Lyon's famed mayor, who wasn't afraid to say that politics was like *andouillette*: "It should smell like dirty toilet, but not too much."

Paco had laughed when he first encountered that line. He didn't think much of tripe sausage either.

The fresco also featured Bocuse's colleagues and friends: François Bise, Jacques Pic, Jean Troisgros, and Alain Chapel, along with Raymond Oliver, depicted in a black-and-white TV because he had once hosted a popular cooking show. There were foreign chefs, too, including Shizuo Tsuji from Japan and James Beard from the United States. Finally, there was Bocuse himself, imperial and debonair.

Paco set up his tripod in front of the first panel and mounted his camera, adjusting the lens to capture every detail. He patiently repeated the operation for each scene. In addition, he shot the explanations written by Bernard Pivot, who was also depicted on the wall—in chef's attire and brandishing a sumptuous cake. The writer seemed delighted to be in such good company.

Paco was putting away his equipment when a man in a chef's jacket emerged from the restaurant and walked over to a bench marked "smoking area." The man, who looked like he was in his twenties, proceeded to stare at the photographer with an intrigued and amused air. When Paco passed him, he asked for a light.

"Sorry, I quit smoking two years ago," Paco answered. "But I have chewing gum, if you'd like."

"No thanks. I've been trying to give up sugar. It's a shame. I burn my fingers all day long in there, and now I don't even have a lighter on me for my cigarette break."

"You work at the restaurant?"

"Yes, I'm a *saucier*. Well, an assistant for now, but I've risen several rungs since getting my start as a kitchen boy, and I intend to climb even higher in the ranks."

"It sounds like the military."

"That's how it works, by brigade. You work up to chef de cuisine—that is, if you've got the guts and the talent. Are you Italian?"

"No, Spanish. From Madrid, but I've lived in France for nearly a decade."

"You have a touch of an accent, but it isn't clear where you're from. You speak very good French."

"Thank you. I had some problems when I arrived, but after I was here for a while, I learned."

"That's often the best way to do it—just jump in and swim. That's what I did."

"You've been here a few years?"

"Yeah, I came from Jerome Thevenay's place in Lyon. My father was a dentist, and he was really disappointed when I told him I wanted to be a chef. He had visions of me becoming a doctor. But he's had nothing but praise for me since I joined Bocuse. He even comes to the restaurant to sample my sauces and stews. That's something, because he's retired now and doesn't have a lot of money."

"He's taking you seriously. I know about that. When my family found out that I wanted to be a photographer, they all predicted I'd be broke and unrecognized. I felt like I had to leave the country just to have faith in my decision. But now that I'm freelancing regularly for a major French publication, they're happy with my choice. They even subscribe to the magazine to see my photos."

"What magazine?"

"*Plaisirs de Table*," Paco said with pride.

"Ah, the glossy rag run by Laure Grenadier."

The man slid over to make room on the bench for Paco.

"She's managing editor, but she writes too. You know her?"

"I saw her a few times at Jerome's restaurant. She's something, that's for sure. Easy on the eyes, and she knows her stuff. But poor Jerome. What an awful way to go. He was a good boss and a great guy. Still, it didn't keep him from being tough when he needed to be. He dressed me down more than once."

Paco set his camera bag on the ground and sat down.

"I didn't have the opportunity to meet him. And his friend Gilles Mandrin—murdered the same way. It sucks."

"I knew Mandrin too. I worked as a temp at his place. He wasn't the same as Jerome—he was more of a joker, a wiseacre. That said, there was no laughing when I was at the stove. Just like Jerome, he could be a taskmaster."

"I can believe that. He fed us the day before he was murdered, and you could tell how much work he put into his food. What a spread that was: loaves of bread, all kinds of pâtés, ham in aspic, pistachio and morel sausage, pork meatballs with spinach…You name it, he had it. I photographed him while we were eating. It's the last portrait ever taken of him, I'm sure."

"Yeah, both Jerome and Mandrin could turn out the food. And the two of them were thick as thieves. They were making big plans together. Did you hear about their bouchon idea?"

"No, I don't believe so."

"They were set on creating a label to differentiate themselves from the other bouchons. What they had in mind was something nice, but also something that didn't take itself too seriously. They wanted to do it with Eric Chevrion, who has a restaurant on the Place du Petit Collège."

"A label? I don't understand."

"You've seen the two stickers. The marionette Gnafron's on both of them. Restaurants that have one sticker or the other always display it in a prominent place. Anyway, Pierre Grison and his Association for the Preservation of Lyonnais Bouchons created the first label twenty years ago and started certifying businesses as authentic bouchons. The Association of Commerce and Industry created the other label five years ago. The point of the labels is letting customers know they're eating at authentic bouchons that meet certain standards. They need the right food and ambiance—that sort of thing."

Paco stretched his arm along the back of the bench and leaned toward the saucier as he continued. Background information like this always helped him when he was taking pictures.

"Grison's label has twenty bouchons, and the other one has twenty-three. The lists change all the time, and certification can be awarded or revoked. But the very top bouchons never get booted off."

"I learn something new every day I'm in Lyon," Paco said, shaking his head. "Who would have thought that restaurants with such humble origins would have their own fancy certifications? I don't know if Mère Guy with her eel stew and open-air place beside the river would be pleased or shocked. Tell me about Chevrion's bouchon. I haven't had a chance to see it yet."

"Chevrion's an asshole. But hey, you've got to give him credit for being a good businessman and having an impeccable menu."

The saucier stood up and dusted off his pants. "Well, enough of this. My break's over. I've got to go."

After a firm handshake, the apprentice returned to the kitchen via the door at the back of the courtyard.

As soon as he disappeared behind the double doors, the photographer searched the inside pocket of his parka for his phone. He pulled it out and discovered he had a message from Laure. He hadn't heard the ping.

"No, all chefs alive and breathing, as far as I know," he tapped into his phone. "But I have some news that's going to interest you. See you tonight."

16

"**O**ne problem down!"

"Is the photographer available?"

"Let's say he is now. When a magazine's as successful as ours, people want to work for it."

Daphne fingered her necklace. Surprisingly, the strands weren't getting tangled in her eight rings. The editorial assistant liked her jewelry, especially pieces made by the artists she hung out with.

"I like your greats-of-culinary-history idea, but I humbly suggest that we get back to what's going on now," she said. "How is your Lyon project coming along? You haven't had much to say about it."

Laure crossed her legs and pulled down her black pencil skirt. "It's had its rewards and its challenges. I love the city, and I've had the opportunity to touch base with chefs I haven't seen for a while. Last night I had chicken poached in pig's bladder at La Mère Brazier. I was out with a newspaper reporter, Jean-Philippe Rameau."

Daphne made a face. "La Mère Brazier notwithstanding, I would have passed on the chicken in the bladder."

"Actually, it was delicious, Daphne." Laure smiled, refusing to share the imagery the chicken had triggered.

"I'll take your word for it. Meanwhile, there must be a pall hanging over Lyon, considering what's happened."

Laure couldn't tell if the editorial assistant's word choice was intentional or an accident.

"That's one way to put it. Let's just say the murders are being felt everywhere."

"Have you been working day and night?"

"Yes and no. You could call my evening at La Mère Brazier a working dinner. My reporter friend had some new information on the cases. But hey, I really enjoyed myself."

"Uh-huh." Daphne winked. "Enjoyed ourselves, did we?"

Laure didn't dignify Daphne's insinuation with a response.

"Tell me more about the chicken. Was it the original recipe?"

"There were some innovations, which were perfectly in line with the spirit of the original dish."

"Was it Mère Fillioux's original recipe or Mère Brazier's?"

"Both. The recipe was created by Mère Fillioux, who wasn't even from Lyon. She was from

Auvergne. She'd slip truffle slices under the skin of the chicken and poach it in a broth of vegetables, fragrant spices, chicken bones, and oxtail. The intense broth was key. Before she dipped the bird in the liquid, she wrapped it in cheesecloth so the fat would stay in the flesh and not get lost in the broth."

"I have to admit, I prefer that to the pig's bladder."

Laure ignored her assistant and continued. "Eugénie Brazier learned the ropes with Mère Fillioux and used the same recipe when she started her own place. But she didn't truss the chicken the same way. Today, Paul Bocuse, her former apprentice, uses the same recipe but poaches the chicken in the pig's bladder instead of cheesecloth. It comes out looking like a big translucent ball the same color as the poultry, and when you pierce it, the chicken appears."

"I love the way ideas transmute as they're passed down," Daphne said. "While we're at it, let's take look at how Ali-Bab made his *poulet demi-deuil*. I bet his recipe is much more caloric. What do you think—three million calories?"

Side by side, the two women opened the book and leafed through the pages until they found the recipe.

For six servings
1) 1 chicken
Veal broth

Truffles at will
Bouquet garni

2) 750 grams stewing veal
250 grams ham
200 grams butter
150 grams heavy cream
125 grams mushrooms
60 grams flour
1 liter consumée
3 medium carrots
2 medium onions
1 bouquet garni
Celery
Salt and pepper

Cook the truffles in Madeira. Poach the chicken
for an hour in the veal broth with the bouquet
garni. Degrease and reduce the broth.

At the same time, prepare a good, fatty béchamel
sauce...

"A fatty-good béchamel sauce," Daphne said.
"Who's not for that?"
They resumed their reading.

As follows: cook the veal, ham cut into pieces
the size of walnuts, and chopped onions, carrots,
and celery in the butter for ten minutes until soft

but not brown. Add the flour and stir for five minutes. Add the consommé, sliced mushrooms, bouquet garni, salt, and pepper. Bring to a boil and lower heat, letting it simmer for two hours. Skim, degrease, strain the sauce, mix it with heavy cream, and heat without boiling until it is thick enough to coat the back of a spoon.

Cut the chicken, set the pieces out on a platter, and coat them with the béchamel sauce to which you have added cooking juices from the chicken and minced truffle. Garnish each piece of chicken with a few truffle slices and serve.

"That will be my reward when I've reached my goal weight," Daphne said, closing the book.

"Fair enough. Just remember—you won't be at your goal weight the day after you eat that dish. We've got to get back to work. And there's one thing I need to tell you."

"What's that?"

"I was planning to do a profile on Jerome Thevenay, but now..."

"Of course. I understand."

"We did an article on him five years ago, with some photos. Could you retrieve it from the archives and pull what we can use for a memorial tribute? We'll do one for Gilles Mandrin too. We have photos taken the day he died. Paco did a great job. Too bad Gilles will never see them."

"That's more work for me, when I'm already drowning! Consider it done, but only in exchange for a little favor, if I may." Daphne pulled an envelope that looked like it contained a CD out of her desk and handed it to Laure. "Can you give this to Paco tonight? He'll know what to do with it."

Laura waited to be in the privacy of her office to take a look. She removed the CD from the envelope. Three voluptuous women were on the cover. Daphne was in the middle, feet firmly planted, looking straight ahead, with the neck of her guitar between her breasts. The other women were on either side of her, with their guitars positioned the same way.

The name of the group was at the bottom: No-Silicone Girls. Maybe no silicone, but lots of leather, tats, and fishnet. Laure grinned. Her talented assistant was a natural.

Laure returned the CD to the envelope just as the screen on her phone lit up. Paco had replied to her text.

17

It was almost ten o'clock when they found themselves in the sitting room of the Hôtel des Artistes. Paco was sipping a beer, and Laure had collapsed in an armchair, her legs stretched out in front of her, her hair up in a messy ponytail.

"I'm beat and not at all hungry," she said.

"You're going to make me eat all by myself?" Paco asked, looking like he was about to sulk.

"Don't give me that face! Frankly, I don't have the energy. I drank green tea on the train, and that will do. Considering everything we've been eating, I don't think I could even stand the smell of food right now."

"Did you wrap up all your loose ends?"

"Yes, our two MIA writers showed up. We re-shot the photos and managed to fill six extra pages. Not bad for one day's work." She yawned loudly and stretched her arms to relax her trapezoids. "And you?"

"I got a lot done. I shot all the frescoes on the Rue des Grands Chefs. I added a few pictures of the courtyard and details of the façade in case you'd like to use them."

"Speaking of which, Daphne wants you to get some shots of the trompe-l'œils in Lyon too."

"She texted me this afternoon. When I finished at Bocuse, I went straight to the Rue de la Martinière and spent the afternoon shooting. We've got all the famous portraits: Abbé Pierre, Bertrand Tavernier, Bernard Lacombe, Claudius and Frédéric Dard, and, of course, Bocuse."

"Perfect! Those murals are a story in themselves. Lyon was a sad, polluted city a half century ago. In 1978, five art students founded a cooperative to design and produce street art. The CitéCréation murals were more than decoration. They traced the history of Lyon, helped residents rediscover their identity, and made art accessible to everyone."

"Noble accomplishments, I'd say."

Laure redid her ponytail. "So, you have some news for me?"

"I didn't want to say anything on the phone." Paco told Laure about his discussion with the young saucier. Laure listened without interrupting and then straightened in her chair, pulling her legs in and folding her hands in her lap.

"If I understand correctly, Thevenay and Mandrin were partnering in the development of a new label. That's hard to believe, considering how

stiff the competition is already. Why create another label and more friction when you could be
working to find common ground?"

Paco shrugged. "I'm just relaying the information. I thought you might find it interesting."

"It is. Two restaurateurs murdered just as they
were launching a new enterprise, one that could
have serious implications for Lyon's restaurant
scene. I'm hoping to set up an interview with
Eric Chevrion at his restaurant, Vieux Sarments.
Perhaps we'll know more soon."

"Did Daphne give you anything for me?"

"Oh yes, I'm sorry. I forgot." Laure rummaged
through her fawn-colored purse and pulled out
the manila envelope containing the CD. Then she
got up to leave. "I'm off," she said. "A hot bath,
some warm tea, and then I'm under the covers
with my laptop."

Laure intended to finish an article she'd e-mail
to Daphne in the morning. She had spent her entire
career in newspapers and magazines, but she had
never liked working against tight deadlines. She
prided herself on her ability to plan, pace herself,
and stay in control. She knew she wouldn't sleep
until she was done.

18

Paco watched Laure get into the elevator, threw on his parka, and left the hotel, heading directly for the Rue de la Mercière, where he had spotted an Eden Rock Café. It was housed in a sixteenth-century mansion that was once one of the city's most exclusive brothels.

He settled in at the bar and scanned the menu. Without hesitating, he chose the double hamburger with bacon and cheddar, fries, salad, and a glass of Côtes du Rhône for the local touch. The server, who had a charming upturned nose, brown curls, and teasing eyes, told him his food would be ready in ten minutes. He swiveled on his stool to watch her walk away.

As expected, the decor was classic mid-century Americana: burgundy leather, dark wood, and gleaming aluminum. The grille of a bright-red fire truck was hanging at the back of the room-- an authentic 1950 Ford with dazzling chrome and sensual curves reminiscent of promise and prosperity. To his left, a wall contained a Hollywood portrait gallery: Humphrey Bogart, Lauren Bacall, Jean Harlow, Clark Gable, Rita Hayworth, and more. Paco would have felt entirely transported from the land of quenelles to a pub-grub place in the United States, were it not for the ubiquitous likeness of Paul Bocuse. A crude representation of the famed chef loomed over a mahogany wall panel. Lyon worshipped the man.

The volume of the music was deafening, but Paco would have turned it up even more to make the most of ZZ Top's "Hey Joe." The rhythmic blues soon gave way to the Rolling Stones and then Neil Young's "Rockin' in the Free World," played on his beloved 1953 Old Black, a Gibson Les Paul Goldtop. Paco closed his eyes, having found his happy place. Born in the first tremors of Madrid's *movida* to a family torn between the nostalgia of Franco's era and the exalted supporters of the republic, he had finally been saved by Christ's love and rock 'n' roll.

His server slammed down a plate and cutlery, jolting him back to reality. The burger was big and juicy, and he threw himself into fully appreciating every bite. When he was done, he licked his fingers and wiped them on his napkin. After drinking the last of his red wine, he let out a contented sigh.

He then picked up a leaflet advertising the live music for the month. The featured groups included the Malabar Sex Toys, the Inglorious Fonkers, the

Tocs, and Daddy No Sleep. Daphne's group would fit right in.

He took the CD from his pocket and glanced at the jacket. The No-Silicone Girls were hot, no doubt about it. With the handle of a Fender Telecaster rising between her breasts, Daphne had impertinently generous dimensions, a sensual smile, and rabble-rousing eyes. Paco couldn't remember the names of the other musicians, but their assets were just as appealing: round hips, soft shoulders, and ample bosoms. He felt a smidgen of guilt, paying so much attention to their looks instead of their musical gifts—which he also appreciated— but who could blame him?

The photographer walked up the stairs to the concert hall. He spotted the man in charge, a lanky fellow in black. Paco slipped him the CD, telling him it was a "great new concept: neo-punk/trash-glamor," and the girls would love to come set fire to Lyon. He said no more and turned around with a wink of complicity that left no room for argument.

Then he exited the Eden Rock without trying to see the waitress, pulled his collar up, and plunged his hands into the pockets of his parka. He left the Rue de la Mercerie, satiated and satisfied at having fulfilled his mission. When he arrived at the Place des Célestins near the hotel, he let out a cavernous burp, releasing a small cloud of onion-smelling steam that rose into the cool night.

19

Lyon's first central market had been set down in the smoking entrails of the Cordeliers district. Built in 1858 under the leadership of architect Tony Desjardins and Senator-Mayor Claude Marius Vaïsse, the building had offered its ample belly to voracious food lovers for well more than a century. In the nineteen seventies, however, the market was deemed unsanitary and torn down, collapsing in a cloud of dust to make way for a parking lot.

The old market was dated and dirty—a health risk even. Still, the people of Lyon felt a void in their hearts. They clung to their images of delivery men on tricycles, flower carts, burdened porters, crowded refreshment stands, overflowing food crates, game hung on hooks, early-morning frostbite, and cheeses threatened by the hot summer sun. Lyon, after all, was a city of food lovers, where some said a fine meal could last a day, starting the day before and continuing to the day after.

So residents were soon crossing the Rhône to a new central market, Les Halles de Lyon at the Cours Lafayette. It was renovated in 2005, and the building, now an imposing glass structure, was renamed Les Halles de Lyon-Paul Bocuse.

Laure couldn't ignore this mecca of food excellence, with its three floors and nearly fifty vendors. Every trip she made to Lyon included a visit. She knew every corner and had put a name to every face. That said, the magazine's archives had only poor images. She intended to fix this with Paco's help. She had gotten him up early and rushed him out of the hotel to get to the market just as the vendors were setting up. She expected photos that were full of life and sensuality.

Paco looked half asleep as they made their way through the quiet streets.

Laure raved about the market's offerings. "Lyon's culinary diversity comes from the wealth of products available in this region. Culinary history depends on geography."

Paco grunted.

"Well, you're in a bad mood this morning, aren't you? That burger with onions must not be sitting well."

He didn't answer.

Laure continued. "Small towns in the area have local specialties. Ampuis grows fine chard. Solaize is known for its leeks. Condrieu produces a small-goat and cow's-milk cheese called *rigotte*. It melts in your mouth when it's young and becomes brittle as it ages. Vaulx-en-Velin has cardoons, so delicious in *gratin de cardons à la moëlle*, with marrow added for extra flavor. Tricastin has black truffles, and the Saône offers small fish perfect for frying."

Paco yawned. Laure was getting annoyed. Still, she wouldn't be discouraged. "There's enough from the areas surrounding Lyon to please the most demanding gourmand. You'll find naturally lean Charolais beef, watercress from Saint Symphorien d'Ozon, and fruits such as Thurins raspberries from the nearby hills, as well as Bresse poultry, frog legs and pike from the Dombes, Vercors honey, pink garlic from the Drôme, Beaujolais and Côtes du Rhône wines, Ardèche sweet chestnuts, and walnuts from Grenoble."

It wasn't until they entered the central market that Paco had anything to say, and it wasn't pleasant.

"You didn't tell me about the damn light in here! You have no idea what a hassle shooting's going to be."

Laure felt like dressing him down but bit her tongue. Getting the photos took priority. "You'll do fine," she said. "Just get started. I'll join you in a minute." Ignoring the noisy tour group planted in front of a neighboring vendor, she leaned over a countertop and ordered a dozen oysters.

Paco stared at her, distaste written all over his face. "I don't know how you can swallow those things so early in the morning."

"It's the best pick-me-up I know of." She turned her back to him, plucked a toothpick from an open jar on the counter, and started in on the winkles that the vendor had thrown into a ramekin to tide her over until the Gillardeau oysters were ready. She needed the salutary effect of iodine to clear her mind of a night filled with bad dreams. A mouthful of the sea and the feeling of being cleaned in the movement of the tide would perhaps erase her visions of coffins and funeral wreaths, gaping pits, and black veils. In a few hours she would have to attend Jerome Thevenay's funeral while everything else seemed to go on as if nothing had happened.

She ate her dozen oysters without lemon, pepper, or shallot vinaigrette. Somewhat refreshed, she retrieved her notebook from her purse, uncapped her pen, and turned into the first aisle to make her rounds. She took her time reviewing the stands, comparing prices, sizing up the presentations, and conversing with the vendors. Occasionally she looked over at Paco, who was focused on piles of fruits, bunches of vegetables, bundles of sausages, and stacks of bread. He seemed to have shed his sour mood and found his stride.

Laure was pleased to see the owners, managers, and vendors from the emblematic houses—Richard cheeses, and Bobosse and Sibilia charcuterie, not to mention Gast catering, Giraudet and Malartre quenelles, Clugnet poultry, and Pupier fish. As she always had before, she stopped to gaze at the shellfish at the stalls of Antonin, Leon, Merle, and Rousseau.

Although the vendors enjoyed chatting with her again, all had been affected by the two homicides. Every person she met brought up the murders. Some said they wouldn't be able to attend Thevenay's funeral but were sending wreaths. Others planned to hang up their aprons early to get to the ceremony.

"We owe him that much," a woman told her. "He was an important member of our community. We miss him already."

Some, their faces tense, admitted they were fearful. "Who's next?" one vendor asked.

Laure shook her head. She couldn't possibly answer the question.

After two hours, Laure, having accomplished as much as she wanted to, went in search of Paco. She found him leaning with his camera over a display of fuzzy mushrooms. She tapped her watch. "Have you seen the time?"

"How could I?" he said. "My eyes have been glued to the camera."

"It's ten thirty. Jerome's funeral begins in less than half an hour."

"Give me two minutes."

"I see you finally got into the swing of things."

Paco looked up from the mushrooms, an apologetic expression on his face. "Sorry I was such a sourpuss. I had no business acting that way. You know the old saying: 'Any day you wake up on this side of the dirt is a good day.'"

20

It was a moving ceremony—simple and sincere, almost like a family gathering despite the overflow crowd. Several representatives of the municipal council and trade associations were there, as well as producers, suppliers, and colleagues of all ages. Laure spotted some of the merchants she had just chatted with, and she guessed that a great number of people who had eaten at Jerome Thevenay's table were also among the mourners.

She slipped away a moment before an organ prelude announced the final hymn and went out to sign the condolence register, open on a lectern covered in black velvet. She jotted some thoughtful words to Jerome's wife, Chloe. As she was writing, she couldn't help but wonder what would become of the restaurant. Would Chloe sell it? Or was there a chance she'd want to run it herself? Now that was a novel idea for the twenty-first century. With less than a handful of exceptions—Bouchon des Filles among them—every bouchon Laure could think of was run by a man. Even Paul Bocuse, who had learned at the knee of the great Mère Brazier, had said he preferred having a pretty woman in his bedroom to having one behind the stove.

Laure shook her head. "*Plus ça change, plus c'est la même chose.*" The more things changed, the more they remained the same.

She quickly added two lines for Cecile, as she wasn't sure she'd see her after the ceremony. An eager crowd of well-wishers would be jostling for access to the family, and Laure didn't want to add to the commotion. She left the incense-filled sanctuary and walked outside for a breath of fresh air.

Saint Bruno les Chartreux was Lyon's only Baroque church. A monastery in the sixteenth century, it had been converted to a parish church after the French Revolution and had undergone many renovations over the years. It was here that, a few years earlier, the funeral Mass for Henri Hugon, one of the most endearing souls in Lyon and a guardian of the city's bouchons, had taken place. Henri had operated Chez Hugon since the nineteen eighties and was known as far away as Paris for his veal blanquette. In fact, some had claimed that Henri's bouchon was the best in Lyon.

Laure looked up at the once-simple front. It had been redone in the nineteenth century by architect Louis-Jean Sainte-Marie, who had given the façade three symmetrical levels. Iconic columns and Doric pilasters flanked the entrance.

Above it was a curved balcony with a window and four fluted columns. A niche containing a statue of Saint Bruno was on the third level.

Laure stepped closer to read the inscription: "Come to me, all you who are laden, and I will give you rest."

A feeling of peace washed over her, but it was short-lived. Inside the church, the funeral recessional rang out. The entrance doors sprang opened, and the coffin, flanked by the pallbearers and followed by the family, emerged from darkness to light. The mourners emerged.

Laure spotted Paco. "You're shivering," he said, joining her. "Here, take my arm."

Laure complied and stared at the people still exiting the church. Two of the last to appear were Cecile's friends, Veronique Lafarqeau in a black sheath and sunglasses and Nathalie Chevrion. Nathalie had a supportive arm around Veronique's waist. It had to be an ordeal for Veronique, Laure thought—attending Jerome's funeral when her own brother, Gilles, had just been murdered too.

Laure watched as the two women walked over to Cecile, who hugged Veronique first and then Nathalie. She averted her eyes, not wanting to intrude on their grief, even from a distance. That was when she saw Nathalie's brother, Eric Chevrion, standing at a distance from the crowd.

There was no mistaking Eric Chevrion. Everything was lean on this closed-faced man in his forties, from his bony hands and dull skin to his thin hair. His sharp eyes made him look willing to attack before being provoked. Laure sensed, however, that under this off-putting appearance, a sensitive person was hiding.

In fact, Chevrion was a shy man who had been insecure his entire life. Behind his stern veneer, he was trying to protect himself. Fortunately, his wife took care of the dining room and the face-to-face with customers. She had an easy smile, a round shape, and a way with words, attributes that allowed Chevrion to stay in his kitchen and avoid his customers. When he did manage to let the sparse hair on his head down, he was given to sarcastic jokes, which were often misinterpreted. One had to know him for some time to grasp his true nature. Jerome, Gilles, and he had been familiar with each other long enough to overcome their differences in personality.

Laure nudged Paco, directing him toward Chevrion. "Eric, how are you?" she asked when they reached him. She looked the chef in the eye without measuring the absurdity of the question.

"How do you think I am?"

"I'd rather be seeing you in different circumstances, as you might imagine. The magazine's doing an issue on Lyon's bouchons, and I've been planning to include yours, as it's one of the best in the city. Could I stop by tomorrow afternoon and sample some of your dishes?"

"Whenever you want. I never go anywhere. I'm there eighteen hours a day."

Indeed, Chevrion was a hard worker, a perfectionist who had spent most of his adult life concocting dishes he wanted to be irreproachable. His veal sweetbread, foie gras *pâté en croûte*, and pig's-ear cake with dried fruit vinaigrette had earned rave reviews.

"Is your wife here?" Laure asked.

"No, she's setting up for lunch service. Somebody has to keep the house running."

"I don't recognize this city anymore. Everything has changed so quickly. I just can't believe what happened to Jerome. And Gilles! We were at Le Gros Poussin three days ago. He opened his kitchen to us, sharing such fine food. He was devastated by Jerome's death, but he had plans. In fact, he mentioned the label the three of you were working on."

Laure had spoken without thinking—lied for that matter. It wasn't like her to get carried away in such an unpremeditated way.

Chevrion's reaction was immediate. His face tightened, and the muscles in his jaw twitched.

Laure feared her totally improvised maneuver was a bit too crass, but she persevered. "It was a good idea," she said in a light tone.

"We always had a lot of ideas whenever we saw each other."

"I guess it's water under the bridge now. Too bad, you could have done something…"

"This isn't the time or place to talk about it," Chevrion snapped.

"I'm sorry. How insensitive of me."

"Tomorrow," he responded coldly, turning on his heel and merging into the crowd.

Paco, looking embarrassed at having witnessed such a rout, cleared his throat. "Um… Laure, you're usually more discreet than that."

"Yes, I didn't handle it with any finesse, did I."

"A bit clumsy, I'd say."

"Well, cut me a little slack, would you? The questions were burning my lips. I want to know more about this project of theirs."

"What are you thinking?"

"Maybe the prospect of a new label was fanning jealousies. Perhaps there were people who wanted to thwart it."

"But would someone kill over a new label—and in that way, with garbage bags, rope, and robberies? It seems a little farfetched."

"The killer could have been trying to disguise his true motive. I'm sure some people know more than they're telling us."

"What about him, over there, hiding out near the cars? Maybe he knows more."

"Is that Tony?"

"Yep, and he's not looking so fresh!"

21

Jerome's *commis de cuisine* was staring at them. His eyes were feverish, and a light salt-and-pepper beard couldn't hide his hollow cheeks. He was wearing an army jacket that was too big for him. The buttons were hanging loose. His jeans were dirty, and his canvas shoes with rubber soles looked like rain-soaked cardboard. Laure and Paco weaved through the crowd and joined him next to the van he was slumped against.

"We should split," Tony whispered. "It smells of cops..."

"What are you talking about?" asked Laure.

"The guy in the corner, near the fence."

"That chubby fellow with the leather jacket?" Paco said. "You really think he's a cop?"

"Yeah, I do. I didn't go talk to the police. I couldn't put myself through their process. I've been hiding out for the past three days, sleeping in my car."

"Since the last time we saw you?" Laure said.

"I went home to get a few things, and then I split. But I had to come out of hiding today. I couldn't miss Jerome's funeral. I had to see him off."

He glanced at the coffin and turned on his heel. Laure and Paco followed suit. They headed toward the Boulevard de la Croix Rousse, where sellers at the open-air market were packing up their merchandise.

"Maybe we shouldn't go this way," Laure said. "There are a lot of people."

Tony sniffed and picked up his pace, throwing furtive glances all around.

"The more crowded it is, the more invisible I am. Don't worry. I know how to do this."

"Where have you been these last few days?"

"Here and there: underground parking garages, dead-end streets in industrial zones. I had some cash on me, but I'm broke now. My car's running on fumes. I left my credit card at home, and I don't want them using it to trace me anyway. I'm sure the cops are watching my house, just waiting for me to show up."

"What can we do to help?"

"Not much... A shower perhaps, I'm beginning to stink."

"And a good meal?"

"I wouldn't say no to that. I'm sick of eating cold food in my car."

"I know a place around the corner—Le Canut et les Gones on the Rue de Belfort," Laure said.

"I'm familiar with it. But maybe you don't want to be seen in a nice place with me, considering how I look."

"We don't care about how you look," Laure answered. "If you're hungry, you need a good meal."

She glanced at Paco.

"What are you doing?" he whispered.

She ignored him. Paco was free to have his doubts, but she believed in Tony.

They reached the Gros Caillou, where the boulevard ended, and veered to the left to head directly to the bouchon. It was early in the service, and there weren't many people. They were shown to a small room to the right of the main dining area.

Paco, having apparently set his concerns aside, looked all around. The restaurant was filled with kitsch, like so many other bouchons. Yet this place was unique. Clocks, photos, and signs filled the dark-yellow walls, some of which were covered with vintage wallpaper. Orange place mats were arranged neatly on all the tables.

As Tony and Laure picked up their menus, Paco reached for the Leica he carried when he didn't have his other equipment. He began shooting.

"I think I'll start with a saddle of rabbit on a bed of spinach and polenta," Laure said, "followed by the croaker with mashed Jerusalem artichokes, leeks, and chestnut chips."

"Too sophisticated for me," Tony muttered. "I need something that'll fill me up."

"So order two main courses: the leg of lamb with roasted potatoes and porcini mushrooms and the rump steak with macaroni gratin. Add a piece of cheese, if you like."

"Sounds good."

"Here, while I'm thinking about it, take this," Laure whispered, slipping a fifty-euro bill under the table.

"I have my pride, but I won't refuse. I'll pay you back."

"No rush."

Paco joined them, and their dishes arrived. Laure could feel Tony relax a little as he began to eat. Sensing he might open up a bit more, she put her fork down and leaned in. "What are you hoping for, hiding like this?"

"That the cops will find the killer and leave me alone."

"Given the stakes, I don't think they're sleeping well. They must be on edge."

Paco took a bite of his pork loin with carrot purée. "This is disastrous for the city's reputation," he said. "They have no choice."

"Paco's right," Laure said. "They must find the murderer. Otherwise, a cloud will always hang over the city."

"Yeah, but what if they frame somebody just to make people think they can go on with their usual lives? That's why I'm playing dead."

Laure didn't respond. She tried another tack. "I spoke with Eric Chevrion at the church."

"I saw you. Talk about under-loved."

"He's not a bad guy. He probably has his reasons for being the way he is."

"A cold fish. I could never stand him."

"I asked him about the label project that Jerome, Gilles, and he were working on. Did you know about it?"

"Their next big thing?"

"The idea's intriguing, but I have the impression there's something more. Chevrion wouldn't answer me. He looked nervous."

"He always looks like that. I don't know why the other two—God bless their souls—got involved. At first, they just wanted to piss off the other labels, which are competitors—you know that. They were out to prove themselves and maybe, if not break the mold, just crack it. It wasn't anything really serious."

"A third label to confuse the food guides?"

"A little, yes. Jerome had started writing a charter. It was a new way of being a bouchon, he said. But you should have seen what Gilles's idea of breaking the mold was: card games and piano and accordion music. Come on."

"And the rumors about some strange guy trying to intimidate the restaurant owners? Do you know anything about that?"

"He's probably feeding the sardines in the port of Marseille. As far as I know, he hasn't been around in years."

"Maybe some old conflict surfaced," Laure said, pouring Tony a glass of Morgon.

"I don't care. For now, I don't want to be involved in any of that crap. I don't know what's going to become of me. I've got no friends, no work, no home... Nothing."

"You have a future in this business, Tony."

"Yeah."

"Your creamed lentils are a marvel. Besides, if Jerome was having you make them, he must have thought yours were better than his. That's something, if you ask me."

Tony shrugged. "I guess so."

"You never wanted to tell us how you make them. There must be a secret."

"Yeah, there is."

Laure reached over and put her hand on his arm. "You can trust me now, can't you?"

"Don't push your luck, Laure. There is a secret, but I'll take it to my grave."

"But if we publish it in our magazine..."

Laure's phone pinged. She pulled it from her purse and looked at the screen: a text from Daphne. "Call me ASAP. It's about Amandine."

22

"**D**on't worry, Laure. She's okay."

Laure had hurried out of the restaurant and was standing on the sidewalk. Her hand trembled as she held the cell phone to her ear.

"Apparently a school chum was having a party at his house in Saclay while his parents were at some conference," Daphne said. "When Amandine got there, all the kids were drinking and making out. She had a drink herself, and a guy started putting the moves on her. At this point she realized she was in over her head. She wanted to leave but was too out of it to know how to get back. You're familiar with Saclay. The transportation's not the best. Thank God, she had her phone and could call me. I went to get her and brought her home with me."

Laure's throat was so tight, she didn't know if she could get her words out. "Why didn't she call me? I'd told her I was in Paris for the day!"

"She knew you'd be heading back to Lyon after you wrapped up things at the office."

"Then why didn't you call me, Daphne? I'm her mother!" Laure waited for an answer, aware that she had never before put Daphne on the spot. Laure didn't know how she'd react, but this was too important.

Daphne cleared her throat. "I apologize, Laure. In retrospect maybe I should have. But I just wanted to get her back to my place and settled. Like I said, she'd been drinking and wasn't feeling so good."

Laure was pacing, taking deep breaths to calm down. "Did anything... Did any of the boys...?"

"No concerns there. She's all right. By the time she was feeling well enough to sleep, it was two in the morning. I didn't want to wake you. You've been working so hard. Then, this morning, I waited until Amandine was up before I called. If I handled it the wrong way, I'm sorry."

Now Laure was sorry. "No Daphne, you did the right thing. I shouldn't have been short with you. Please forgive me."

"No need to apologize, Laure. I understand completely. I have nieces. And the stories I could tell you—"

Daphne always knew how to break the tension, but Laure wasn't ready to hear any stories about adolescent escapades. "I don't understand, Daphne. Amandine was staying with her father while I was gone. Why didn't she call him? I can't imagine him allowing her to go to an unsupervised party."

"Apparently he's out of town too. He's spending a few days in Sancerre with his new girlfriend, visiting the villages and wine cellars."

Laure felt the heat rise to her cheeks again.

"You mean Nathan took off with a new girlfriend and didn't tell me? He was supposed to be taking care of Amandine!"

It took Daphne awhile to respond. "I'm just glad I was able to get her, and nothing happened. We stopped at your place to pick up her pajamas, bookbag, and some clothes, and she's had something to eat. I'm working from home to keep an eye on her. Do you want me to give Amandine the phone?"

"Yes."

Laure waited while Daphne went into another room to get her daughter. She shifted to box breaths, counting five on the inhale, five holding, five on the exhale, and five again before inhaling again. She felt her muscles let go of some of the tension.

Amandine was on the phone a moment later. "Mom, I'm so sorry!" She sobbed.

Laure let her cry.

"I was stupid," Amandine finally said, sniffling.

"Yes, that was a stupid thing to do. What would we have done if Daphne hadn't come to get you? Amandine, if anything had happened to you…"

"I know, Mom. I won't do anything like that ever again. I promise."

A couple emerged from the restaurant, laughing had chatting. Laure picked up the faint odors of meat, rosemary, and thyme on their jackets before turning her back and stepping away to keep them from hearing.

"I'll have to talk with your father. You were supposed to be with him. I have a hunch you never went to his place. Am I right?"

Amandine was silent.

"Amandine, I need to know."

"Yes," Amandine said, her voice barely a whisper.

"So, you went to a party I didn't know about in a place you couldn't get home from, and you lied to both your father and me."

"Yes."

"All right, we'll talk about this when I get home. Put Daphne on the phone again, please."

Laure heard the phone pass hands. "You're okay with her staying with you until I get back?"

"Of course, Laure."

"Thank you, Daphne. You're a lifesaver. I can't bear to think of what could have happened to her."

"Well, it didn't, and I think she'll learn from this. Kids that age are hard to deal with. They're too young to know what they're doing, and they have too many opportunities to get into trouble. But you're a good mom. You two will figure this out."

Laure thanked Daphne one more time and said good-bye. It had been a wakeup call. She had to do a better job of coordinating with Nathan. But more important, she would work on her relationship with Amandine. The girl had become more distant, and Laure had chalked it up to ordinary adolescence. Maybe going to wild parties was ordinary adolescence these days, but it wasn't what she intended for her daughter. She needed to know what was going on in Amandine's life, and she wanted her daughter to trust her. That was how it was when Amandine was younger. It would be that way again.

Laure dropped her phone in her purse, lifted her chin, and walked back into the restaurant.

23

The papers had moved on from the murders. With nothing new to report, the chef homicide articles were now relegated to the inside pages. On the front page, the Olympique Lyonnais soccer team, one of the most popular first-division soccer clubs in the country, was getting all the attention and the seventy-two-point headlines. They were playing at home that night.

Paco folded the paper, annoyed that Laure had accepted Cecile and Francois Frangier's dinner invitation for both of them. He wouldn't be able to take in this soccer high mass. Paco was a true fan of Real Madrid, but that didn't keep him from appreciating other exceptional teams playing under different colors.

A minute later he heard Laure in the lobby, and he could tell by the determined click of her boot heels that they were in for another nonstop day.

She had seemed preoccupied after taking the call from Daphne the previous afternoon, and he hadn't asked any questions. Claiming fatigue, Laure had cancelled their last interview and photo session, and they had returned to the hotel.

"I won't be eating out tonight," she had told him before going up to her room. "You can do whatever you'd like."

And that's what Paco had done. He looked at his watch and decided he could still spend an hour or two at the Musée des Beaux-Arts, housed in a seventeenth- and eighteenth-century Benedictine convent. Once there, he headed straight for the treasured sculptures, including Rodin's *The Temptation of Saint Anthony*, Bourdelle's *Carpeaaux at Work*, Maillol's *Venus*, and Pradier's *Odalisque*.

Paco took pride in his photography, but he secretly wished he had a sculptor's gift. He was in awe of the way the famed artists could capture the muscles, curves, and dynamics of the human form.

After the museum closed, he had taken a long walk and snapped additional photos—for himself, not the magazine—and he, too, had called it an early night.

This morning, he was grateful for the few extra hours of sleep he had gotten. Laure was all business again. She had fallen behind schedule, and that wasn't good. Laure was compulsive about time management, and one way or another, she'd make up for what she had lost. Paco figured the best course of action was keeping his mouth shut, as he had the day before.

They first ascended the Fourvière Hill, atop which Christian Têtedoie's storied restaurant was perched—on the site of the former Antiquaille hospital. Laure was adamant that he figure in the next issue. She was planning to honor him and Mathieu Viannay in a special sidebar, a reminder that Lyon had other prestigious chefs outside the Bocuse constellation.

The welcome couldn't have been warmer. Têtedoie answered her question without hesitation, gave up some of his secrets, had them taste new dishes, and pointed Paco to interesting perspectives from the terrace, which overlooked the whole city. The view was majestic, the refinement of the dishes flawless, and the furniture and tableware chosen with taste. Laura seemed to relax.

Paco loosened up too. Sautéed foie gras with rich-smelling guanaja chocolate and *fleur de sel* and *boudin noir* with apples and calvados helped him slough off any morning preoccupations. Now everything was fine.

The photographer shot a beautiful portrait of the chef in his white jacket with red-and-white trim, certifying that he had received the prestigious Meilleur Ouvrier de France. This uniquely French award had been created in 1924 with the objective of reviving the country's traditional crafts. It was a fierce competition requiring many months— sometimes years—of preparation. Holding the title confirmed refinement and excellence in technical skills, innovation, and respect for tradition. It was a lifetime award.

While Paco took his photos, Laure, more calorie-conscious, tasted the *cassoulette de légumes* and steamed sea bass with roasted beetroot and a vegetable emulsion.

When they left the restaurant, their curiosity and senses satisfied, Laure looked at her watch.

"We told Eric Chevrion that we'd stop at his place today, but I don't think we can fit it in. We have too many other people to see. I'll call when we get back to the hotel, make our apologies, and reschedule for tomorrow, after we meet with the poultry farmer."

They devoted the rest of the day to handpicked artisans, including bakers, cheese makers, butchers, caterers, pastry chefs, and confectioners. They had no time to interview everyone on their list, but Paco promised to return to shoot all of them. They also made a few incursions into smaller restaurants, from which Laure emerged somewhat disenchanted by the average quality of the chow.

On their way back to the Hôtel des Artistes to freshen up for dinner with the Frangiers, Laure insisted on one final stop—at La Pince ou La Cuisse, which specialized in crayfish and frogs. They had barely crossed the threshold when they felt the wave of animosity.

"Ah, the return of the Parisians!"

"That's quite a welcome!" Laure replied, smiling warily.

"What did you expect me to say? So good to see you again? I don't easily forget, madam!"

"Good afternoon would suffice."

"You don't recall your article 'Lyon: The Best and the Worst,' do you?"

"The headline wasn't the best. I grant you that."

"Who cares about the headline? It's the content of the article that left a bad taste in my mouth."

"I don't remember everything in that piece. If I recall, we ran it two or three years ago."

"Let me refresh your memory: 'The crayfish was drowning in its carcass. The flesh had the consistency of cotton.' And even harsher: 'Even if the frog's dead, its legs should be sautéed with more consideration.'"

"If you're recounting it, I must have written it," Laure said.

"It was under your byline!"

"I write it as I experience it. I'm sorry if it was painful for you."

"Painful? It was worse than that. You nearly killed us. Our business took a thirty percent hit. We had to let some of our wait staff go. And we still haven't made up for what we lost."

Seeing how worked up the restaurant owner was becoming, Paco felt a protective urge to step in. But one look at Laure, and he knew it wasn't necessary. She was quite capable of handling this herself.

"I've always been sincere and honest in my articles," she said calmly. "I write what I think without prejudice, and I never promise anything. It's not my style to be lukewarm or reserved. I like it, or I don't like it."

"Well, we're similar then. And I don't like you—not in the least."

"Let me add, monsieur, that I'm back today to see where you stand now. Being a specialized bouchon isn't easy. I've heard your restaurant has improved, and if that's the case, I'll tell our readers."

"And I should trust you when you've already tried to kill me?"

"Don't be so melodramatic. If it's good, everyone will know."

"And tell me: what difference will that make if I'm suffocated in a garbage bag before your precious magazine comes out?"

24

Laure and Paco left the bouchon on that sober note and returned to the hotel to change their clothes. Laure rescheduled with Eric Chevrion, who, although irritated, agreed to see them the following day. They arrived at Cecile and François Frangier's place after nightfall. Amber light from the chrome lamps flanking the white-linen sofas warmed the living room.

Laure was feeling more like her old self. She had checked in with Daphne, and her editorial assistant had assured her that both her daughter and the magazine were fine. She still needed to hash things out with Nathan, but she would get to that tomorrow—she wanted a little more time to gather her wits.

Laure surveyed the comfortable apartment again, taking in the overall effect and the individual pieces, all of which had clearly been chosen with care. She walked over to the dining area and brushed her fingers across the rustic tabletop, mounted on contemporary wrought-iron legs.

"It's mango wood," François said. "Cecile and I try to go sustainable whenever we can. It's hardwood from Southeast Asia, and it's easy to work with. But unlike the big towering trees in Europe and the United States, which take as long as fifty years to mature, mango trees reach their peak in fifteen years or so. When they get too tall or stop bearing fruit, they're harvested for lumber, and new trees are planted."

"François is very keen on saving the earth," Cecile said.

"Then we are of the same mind," Paco said. "Madrid, my home city, has instituted an electric bike-sharing program to cut down on traffic. It had some glitches at first, but I understand it's working well now."

"That's good to hear," François said. "I used to enjoy cycling. Can't do much these days, though. My knee gives me too much trouble."

François got up and walked over to a bar tucked in a corner of the room. "Well, my friends, can I fix you drinks?"

Cecile also got up. "If you'll excuse me, I need to duck into the kitchen to check on our *petits fours*."

Laure turned her attention back to François. "Just sparkling water for me, thanks."

"Are you sure you don't want something stronger?" he asked. "I have a nice bottle of Vega

Sicilia Unico, which I bought when Cecile told me Paco was coming too."

"Sparkling water's fine, believe me. We've been putting in some long hours, and I won't make it through the evening if I start drinking."

"It's up to you." He gave the water to Laure and poured a glass of Unico for Paco. "It's aged in oak longer than any other wine. I think you'll like it." Returning to his chair, François started to hand Laure a Limoges bowl filled with pistachios. "Would you like some of these?"

Paco grabbed the bowl before she could take it. "Don't mind if I do!"

Laure couldn't believe it. Chagrined, she tried to recover. "Paco loves pistachios," she said with a smirk. "He trains with them regularly."

Cecile returned to the room, carrying a platter of perfectly golden puff pastries. "What did I miss?" she said, sitting down.

Laure didn't answer. "I hope you didn't go to too much trouble making a meal for us," she said after a moment.

"Not to worry. Cooking relaxes me, and, after all, life must go on. I went to the police station this afternoon to give my statement. It felt good to talk with them freely. Maybe something I said will help them find the murderer."

Laure nodded. "Have you had a chance to talk to Chloe about her plans for the restaurant? Would she want to run it herself?"

Cecile sighed. "Chloe has no interest in cooking. She'd feed her children frozen dinners every day of the week if she could get away with it. You've heard the proverb about the cobbler's children with no shoes? Jules and Marie-Anne are the chef's kids with no fresh vegetables."

"Then she'll be selling?"

"Most likely. I'm sure she won't have trouble finding a buyer. Veronique told me just today that someone had already shown up at her brother's restaurant to inquire about a sale."

Laure glanced at Paco. "Do you think it was the same man who came around awhile ago?"

"I couldn't tell you, Laure." Cecile picked up a puff pastry and raised it to her mouth. "At any rate, I'll be getting back to our store soon."

"Take your time, honey," François said, his voice gentle. "There's no rush. I can handle the store alone."

"That's right," Laure said. "You have to take care of yourself. The subject must come up with customers. It may be better to stay away for a while."

François lifted his arms, as if appealing to a higher power. "You don't know how right you are, Laure. There's no way around it. Tact isn't everyone's strong suit. It's different for chefs and restaurant owners. They need to relieve their anxieties. But other people—they're just curious. I propose that we drop the subject, for now at least. How about that soccer match that's coming up tonight? Do you like *futball*?"

François was asking Paco, which, despite her lack of interest in the sport, vexed Laure.

"He loves it so much, it's appalling," she answered for him.

Now it was Paco's turn to be embarrassed. "As a matter of fact, I am a fan. I used to play."

"Oh? What position?"

"Goalie," Paco said, staring at Laure. "I'm good at catching things."

"No doubt about it, a great goalie's hard to find," François said. "You need sharp reflexes and the ability to judge angles. You've got to be a risk-taker too. Kind of like being a photojournalist, wouldn't you say?"

"I'd say." Paco was still looking at Laure.

"I'm an OL fan, always and forever," François said, oblivious to the exchange.

"That's Olympique Lyonnais—OL."

Laure glared at her photographer.

"If you'd like, you could stay after dinner, and all four of us could watch the game together," François said.

Laure already knew how Paco would respond. From the looks of their apartment, François and Cecile probably had a 65-inch flat screen hidden somewhere. How could it compare with the relatively tiny television in his hotel room?

"That's a great idea!" Paco enthused while Laure did her best to appear agreeable. "The TVs in our rooms are so small, the players look like ants. How could I refuse?"

Cecile, probably sensing that her guests weren't on the same page, changed the subject. "Shall we eat?" she said, motioning Laure, Paco, François toward the dining area.

She went into the kitchen and returned with a large terracotta dish containing a lamb tagine wafting sweet and spicy aromas. She placed it on the table, and they all sat down.

As they ate, Laure complimented Cecile on the melt-in-your-mouth meat, the subtle fragrances, and the perfect texture of the vegetables. Cecile told her that the firmest vegetables had been added first, and then the softer ones, based on the time they needed to achieve the perfect doneness.

"How long does the whole dish take?" Laure asked. "Two hours?"

"Almost three on low heat," Cecile said. "You really need to give the spices time to permeate the meat, vegetables, and sauce."

"And everything should be chopped just right," François added. "You must never forget the importance of proper knives."

A lengthy history of the family business followed. François's grandparents had started a knife-making venture in the Auvergne region, and his parents continued to run it after the death of the grandparents. François, in turn, inherited the business and moved it to Lyon. But it subsequently experienced a downturn, as buyers began switching to lower-grade and less-expensive knives.

That was when Cecile, now married to François, stepped in. She reimagined the business as a tableware retailer and was largely responsible for its success. Cecile was talented and energetic. She stocked the store with the finest porcelain china and Baccarat crystal from France, table linens from Italy, colorful textiles from Central America, and one-of-a-kind bowls, mugs, trays, and serving pieces thrown by regional artisans.

Laure knew the story by heart and was listening with one ear. The hostess eventually interrupted her husband, whose monologue was dragging on.

"Well, it looks like we're finished with our tagine. I'll go back into the kitchen and prepare dessert. I have a surprise for you, Laure."

"Just for me?"

"Yes, I know you'll love it."

"I love so many things. I couldn't possibly guess what it is."

"I need a little time to add the finishing touches, but it will be ready before the start of the game."

Paco leaped up before Cecile had even pushed back her chair. "Let me help you clear the table," he nearly yelled. And with the theatricality of a server in an upscale restaurant, he placed two plates on his forearm and cried out, "*Chaud devant.*" No sooner had he followed Cecile into the kitchen than Laure and François heard a crash, a string of expletives in Spanish, and many apologies in French.

Paco emerged from the kitchen, tagine sauce dribbling down his pants.

"Everyone, stay here while I clean up," Cecile said, trailing him out. Her face was flushed, and her shoes and pants were covered with sauce. "I don't need any help cleaning up. What I need is some peace and quiet to do my dessert." She turned on her heel and went back into the kitchen.

François handed Paco a linen napkin. "At times like this, it's better to be invisible."

Paco wiped off his pants, a sheepish look on his face. He tossed the napkin on the table, and François ushered them into the den, where, as Laure had expected, a large flat screen was mounted on the wall. Taking care to keep his pants from touching the upholstery, Paco settled into a chair while Laure glared at him.

The game hadn't started yet. Instead, there was a retrospective of the team's best years and players, including Juninho Pernambucano, a fearless attacking midfielder from Brazil. He joined OL in 2001 and stayed for eight years, helping the team win seven consecutive league titles.

"Rather gifted for a guy who doesn't use his hands," Laure said.

Paco didn't answer right away. "Gifted is an understatement," he finally said. "He's the greatest dead-ball specialist of all time."

François didn't seem to be listening to his guests any longer.

"Whatever that means," Laure said. "In any case, he's hot—beautiful eyes, sensual mouth, firm behind, broad muscular chest, strong arms—"

Paco cut her off. "And retired, married, the father of three children, and living in Brazil."

"Nothing wrong with admiring the menu. They all look pretty good, if you ask me."

A sportscaster was interviewing the coach, and the camera was panning the stands, where fans had begun shouting and singing.

Cecile arrived, belting out the lyrics of the same song. She was carrying a platter with four plates, each with a perfect chocolate mousse dome set on a base of speculoos cookies and topped with a mocha sauce.

Laure, startled by the show of OL spirit, stared at Cecile. "I never knew you could sing, Cecile."

"Indulge me," she said, dabbing her eyes before slicing the cake. "Jerome loved the team too."

25

Laure got up earlier than usual the next morning. She wanted to get her talk with Nathan out of the way before Paco and she embarked on their drive to the poultry farm in Bourg-en-Bresse. Laure had learned long ago that it was best to have serious discussions with her ex on her own time and her own terms. Nathan had never been an easy man.

He picked up on the third ring, sounding wide awake.

"Hello, Nathan. I assume I didn't get you up."

"No, not at all, Laure. I've been up for hours. I got my run in, and I've already showered."

Wasn't that just like Nathan. Up and running when he could be snuggling with his new girl-friend. Laure almost laughed. All right, maybe the girlfriend was a runner too.

"What's up, Laure?"

Laure plunged in. "I'm calling about Amandine. She got herself into a jam, and I found out that she wasn't with you. I'm out of town, and she told me she'd called you and made arrangements to stay at your place."

"What kind of jam, Laure? And no, she never talked to me. I'm shocked that you didn't call me yourself. In fact, I was out of town too."

Laure winced. Yes, she knew now that she should have called Nathan. She had trusted her daughter more than she should have. Laure would take the rap this time, but she wouldn't let her ex convict her.

"Our daughter went to a party where all the kids were drinking and screwing around, and she couldn't get home on her own."

"Is she all right? How could you allow this to happen?"

"She's okay, Nathan. She's with Daphne. And it happened because she lied. I'm not being overly harsh. She's a kid. It's to be expected. Still, her dishonesty is upsetting, and we have to rethink how much supervision she needs."

"Laure, I knew it would come to this sooner or later. You've allowed your job to take over your life. When you're not in the office, you're traveling, and Amandine has suffered for it. You don't know where she is, who she's hanging out with... And what about her grades? Have they dropped too? Maybe we need to revisit our custody arrangement."

Ah, yes. Some things were predictable—or rather, some people. Laure had met Nathan in her early twenties. They were both establishing themselves: she as a food writer and he as a cardiologist. Soon they were married, and Laure was thrilled when she learned she was pregnant. Although Nathan wanted her to quit her job when Amandine was born, she resisted and took a three-month leave. But soon it was time to go back to work, and truth be told, Laure was more than ready.

Instead of being supportive and helpful at home, Nathan left all the shopping and cooking to Laure, despite her long hours. When Laure refused to quit her job to work from home, Nathan made her feel guilty for not having market-fresh food and homemade meals for their child.

Nathan's desire to control her had never abated. He chided her when he thought she was eating too much or not doing the dishes correctly. He never read her newspaper or magazine articles. Neither did he celebrate her promotions, which, despite her deteriorating home life, were coming in quick succession.

At the beginning, Laure had adored Nathan. He was smart and charming. He had lavished her with gifts and phone calls and couldn't wait to see her. He was an ardent lover. And good-looking, with olive skin, curly black hair, hazel eyes, and lips that invited kisses. Laure had been swept up.

After a few years of marriage, however, she felt like dust under his feet. Laure still remembered the day she called her mother in tears.

"Laure, I've bitten my tongue, but I won't do that any longer," her mom had said. "Nathan was never right for you. He's too much, and you're too independent. You don't need this. It's not good for Amandine either."

It was exactly what Laure needed to hear. Within a week, she was seeing a therapist. A few months later, she served Nathan with divorce papers. How shocked he was!

The days when her ex could push her buttons and put her on the defensive were long past. Sitting on the bed in her hotel room, Laure waited, making sure Nathan was finished.

"Nathan, I understand that you're concerned about Amandine, as I am," she said in a voice as calm as a counselor's. "I agree that I should have coordinated her visit with you, and I'll be vigilant about that in the future. I also intend to spend more time with her. She needs the same from you. Both of us must be more involved in her life, and it's imperative that we work together. Why don't we sit down and figure this out, the two of us?"

There was a pause at the other end. Laure sensed that Nathan was weighing his response.

"All right, Laure. When you get back to Paris, give me a call, and we'll set up a time."

Laure said good-bye. Smiling, she tossed the phone on the bed. She got up and walked into the bathroom to brush her teeth. She had twenty minutes to get dressed and meet Paco.

In truth, she had never regretted marrying Nathan. After all, look what she had to show for it: Amandine.

26

The Japanese rental smelled of new plastic. The hatchback had neither charm nor character: gray exterior and black interior. But it did have some features—standard in many cars—that Paco liked, including a rearview camera, collision warning, a slick navigation system, and a curb monitor. If he'd been on his own, he would have chosen a jazzier car. But he wasn't. He was with Laure.

His boss hated cars and insisted on going at one speed—slow. She had gotten her driver's license by some stroke of luck but had never needed it because she lived in Paris.

"Didn't you ever consider getting a car?" he had asked her once.

"No. Of course, Nathan had a car when we were married. But I didn't rely on it that much. The metro, buses, and taxis were always available, and I love walking. When Amandine was a baby, I wore her."

"You wore her?"

"Yeah, it's this cloth thing you wrap around you and put the baby inside. It's quite handy."

"I'll take your word for it."

For out-of-town trips, Laure almost always traveled by rail or plane. Paco wondered if she could even find her driver's license anymore. He glanced at her and was surprised to see a pensive look on her face. She had been so cheerful when she slipped into the passenger seat.

"Paco, could you turn the radio down, please?"

He complied, staying focused on the road.

"Could you just turn it off?"

Paco complied again and silenced Linkin Park. "Anything wrong?" he asked.

"No, we've got everything under control. But I have to admit I'm concerned about Tony. I'm thinking about Gilles Mandrin, too. His funeral arrangements haven't been announced yet, and I'm wondering if I can attend. We have a lot on our plates."

"Yes, we do."

"We'll leave for Paris tomorrow night, and you can return to Lyon to finish up the portraits of the artisans."

"You won't be coming back?"

"You'll do fine without me. We still have problems with the current issue. We've got to make it to press on time. Besides, I know all those people, and I don't need to see them again. I'll put together a list with their names, addresses, and phone numbers so you can set up your shoots."

"When do I get to come back?"

"After you've reshot our shrimp. Daphne dug up another photographer, but we've never worked with him before, and considering everything that's gone wrong already, I'm not about to tempt fate."

"But I heard he was a good photographer," Paco said.

"Perhaps, but I'd still rather use you."

"And how do you want your artisans?"

"Some are Meilleur Ouvriers de France. They should be in their professional attire with the tricolor collar."

"Okay. No worries."

"Yes, but your portraits must convey their pride in what they do and their talents. These are gifted people who've worked hard to get where they are, and they continue to work like crazy. We must honor them."

Paco nodded.

Laure continued. "For the butchers, you'll need Alexandre Baronnier, who has taken over the reins at the Boucheries André. He's a third-generation head of the company. Then there's Eric Cochet at Bresse. At the Boucherie Centrale, make sure you get Samuel Perrier and Nadège Giraud. At Bucherie Trolliet, you'll want Maurice Trolliet and his son Alexis and daughter-in-law Laurence. Maurice has been a butcher since he was seventeen.

He's one of a kind. But they're all fascinating—artists in their own right."

"Sounds like it," Paco said.

"Many of these people are heads of sizable businesses, but breaking down meat is their stock-in-trade, and they spend years perfecting their skills in preparing, cutting, trimming, chopping, and boning. One day I'll explain."

"Meat shots can be tough, but I'll do my best."

"I have faith in you, Paco."

"You need the right angle and the right lighting. Otherwise, a photo can make a reader queasy."

"That may be, but when a piece of marbled beef or a slightly pink rack of lamb arrives at my table, I'm drooling."

Having reached the outskirts of Bourg-en-Bresse, they took another road into the countryside. Ten kilometers later, they arrived at the well-appointed Deloiseau farm, which specialized in traditionally raised free-range Bresse poultry. The owner, Louis Deloiseau, welcomed them warmly, as an article in the magazine was the sign of long-awaited recognition.

The visit followed the usual protocols: caps and masks made of hygienic paper and over-shoe protection. After touring the laboratories, they lingered in the breeding areas and were treated to a lengthy explanation of the chickens' diet, fattening practices, banding, and nail trimming. Paco shot nonstop, kneeling in the grass to capture the hens at eye level and winding up with feathers all over his shirt and pants.

"I didn't get anything on my pants, did I?" he whispered to Laure on their way back to Louis's office. "Even with the masks, the smell can be overpowering."

Grinning, Laure sniffed, looked him over, and shook her head. "You're fine."

When they reached his office, Louis couldn't resist the urge to show off his trophies and diplomas. Laure paused in front of a charcoal drawing of a nineteenth-century gentleman with a well-groomed beard, thick eyebrows, and shiny hair. He was sitting at a desk with an air of nobility.

"Is he one of your ancestors?" she asked.

"Not at all. You have before you the most glorious defender of the Bresse chicken, the great poet Louis-Gabriel-Charles Vicaire, twice crowned by the Académie Française."

"I can't say I've heard of him."

"He died in 1900, and, believe me, it's hard to find poets of his caliber these days. Listen to this beautiful poem." Louis picked up a worn leather-bound book he didn't need to open, as he obviously knew the poem by heart. "It's called 'La Poularde'."

Paco suppressed a laugh. Marc Chagall and René Magrite had painted chickens, but he had never heard of a poem called "The Hen."

Louis recited:

Naive child of Bresse,
So succulent and honest
To those who settle you in a
thin white fat nest,

Cousin of the bountiful men
Who in our land abound,
Far from ungrateful,
In our family, you are crowned.

Louis then reeled off a string of rhymes about respectable paunches, heavy eaters, and the sin of gluttony. He declaimed them, nearly licking his chops, and went on with the final verse.

Were my pastor to blame me
until my last hour,
O spring chicken,
My love for you would not sour!

Laura and Paco thanked him awkwardly, and Louis Deloiseau, whose flushed cheeks betrayed his emotion, suggested that he recite "Le Chapon," another ode Vicaire had written in a dozen quatrains. They declined, saying they had an urgent meeting in Lyon and a long drive back. But they promised to return. Louis reluctantly let them go, the book still open in his hands.

They waited until they reached the main road before breaking out in laughter.

"If we had stayed any longer, we would have heard a poem about every farm animal in France," Paco said, still laughing as he turned on the radio. To the beat of a Jay-Z hit, he began rapping out odes to pigs, turkeys, and hedgehogs, with Laure howling at each increasingly smutty rhyme.

Paco accelerated without any reproach from Laure. He looked at her and saw that she was wiping away her tears of laughter. It was good to see her relaxed and unconcerned about her work.

As they approached Lyon, he switched to another station and listened to the weather forecast. Light rain was predicted. The traffic reporter warned drivers of a delay on the northern bypass. Then the local news resumed, with what had most likely been the lead story earlier in the day. Eric Chevrion, chef at Les Vieux Sarments, had been found dead in the back room of his restaurant.

27

"Come on," Laure yelled into the phone, which she had switched to speaker. "Answer!"

The radio report hadn't given more than the bare bones. Laure had switched to the other local stations, only to hear the same basics: a third homicide at a third bouchon. Nothing more.

Then she had pulled out her cell phone and called Jean-Philippe. It took him six rings to pick up.

"Yes, Laure. I'm assuming you've heard."

"It's horrible!"

"Murdered like the others."

"Are you still working the homicides?"

"Obviously."

Jean-Philippe was back to being cool with her. Laure gave Paco a sidelong glance and couldn't miss the gleeful smile on his face. He could tell the man wasn't giving her anything. But she wouldn't be put off. She changed strategy.

"Do you know about the label?"

"Why do you ask?"

"You do know."

"Vaguely, but why are you asking about it now?"

"Because Jerome Thevenay, Gilles Mandrin, and Eric Chevrion were putting together this new label."

"Who told you?"

"That doesn't matter. The label links the three homicides. Jerome, Gilles, and Eric weren't just three random bouchon owners."

"Have you told the police?"

"No, I had no reason to believe that Chevrion would be murdered too."

"Of course."

"Do you... Do you know how he was killed? Was it the same method?"

"Where are you calling from?" Jean-Philippe sounded annoyed. "Are you in a car? I'm having trouble hearing you."

"Paco and I are on our way back from Bourg-en-Bresse."

"Look, I'm in a café on the Rue Saint Jean. Join me." Jean-Philippe ended the call without waiting for an answer.

Stunned by the news, Laure and Paco were silent for the last twenty kilometers of the drive. As they approached the city's historic center, the streets became congested. The police had cordoned off the area around Les Vieux Sarments and were doing their best to control a crowd that seemed more curious than worried. Cars had slowed to a crawl.

Laure called Jean-Philippe again. "I'm going to have trouble reaching you. There are tons of people around the crime scene, and some of the streets are blocked."

"Where are you now?"

"In front of the Maréchal Juin bridge."

"Okay. Tell Paco to drop you off at the docks just before the courthouse. I'll come to you."

Laure told Paco what to do. She saw that he wasn't pleased about leaving her, but he did as she asked and said he'd return the rental car.

As Laure stepped out of the vehicle, she spotted Jean-Philippe walking toward her, his face a mix of concern and anxiety.

"Thanks for coming to meet me," she said when he reached her. "I have to admit this last death has really shaken me up. I'm a bundle of nerves."

She was about to regret showing her vulnerability when she saw the look on Jean-Philippe's face. He was hungrily sizing her up, responding, it seemed, to her openness. Had she misjudged his tone on the phone? Maybe he was distracted, busy calling his sources. It was understandable. She sometimes put people off when she was working on a story. Laure relaxed a little and allowed him to take her elbow.

"We'll go this way and avoid the crowds," he said.

They walked a few meters toward the cordoned area and stopped in front of a small ironwork door that Jean-Philippe opened.

"Follow me," he ordered.

He led her to a passageway that opened into a courtyard framed by Renaissance buildings. Laure admired the arched walkways, columns, and rounded turret rising several stories high. Jean-Philippe didn't take any notice and pointed her to a second passageway to the Rue des Trois Maries. He waited a moment, his hand on a heavy door. Then he nodded, and they came out into the open again. At the end of the street, the crowd was becoming more agitated. Clearly, the rumors were flying. Jean-Philippe hustled Laure into another building. At the entrance to the courtyard, she stopped to admire a spiral staircase that seemed to climb to heaven.

Jean-Philippe put a hand on her shoulder. "Don't tell me you didn't know about the city's secret passageways, the *traboules.*"

"Of course, I know about them," she answered. "Who doesn't? They're an old-city tourist attraction. But I've never been in them before. They're incredible."

"Lyon has a lot of incredible things. All you need is me to guide you."

Jean-Philippe's phone pinged. He consulted his text message and suggested that they exit through the Rue Saint Jean, returning to the café where he had set up makeshift headquarters. "How did you find out about the label?" he asked, helping her into her chair.

"First, you tell me something about the third murder. Same MO?"

"You're really interested in these homicides, aren't you?"

"You sound surprised. I'm an editor of a food magazine, and the people who've been murdered are well-known chefs. Doesn't it stand to reason that I'd be interested?"

Jean-Philippe was quiet for a moment and then nodded. "Okay, I'll tell you what I have, but you're not to write anything about it."

"We're not a news publication, Jean-Philippe. I just need to know."

Jean-Philippe pushed his notebook aside and leaned forward, his elbows on the table. "According to the police, this homicide was similar but not identical: three blows to the head instead of one. Chevrion was choked, and his head was stuffed in a freezer bag, not a garbage bag. His hands and feet were bound with heavy kitchen twine, rather than rope. Cash was stolen, but the killer left the coins, gift cards, and checks."

"Why was this one different?" Laure asked, eager for more information. "Do you think someone or something interrupted the killer or forced him to change his plans?"

"The police aren't saying. I don't think they know yet, anyway."

"Could it be a message? Is the murderer trying to make us understand something?"

Jean-Philippe shook his head. "No way to tell at this point. The police just hope it isn't a copycat looking for attention."

"That's crazy!"

"They can't rule it out. The situation is becoming unmanageable. The police are on edge, and the prefect is on the verge of apoplexy. I was lucky to get this much out of them. I just hope my editor understands that I'm working as hard as I can. He's like a bear that needs to be fed every morning. He comes into the office sniffing the air, and you'd better have some fresh meat."

"No wonder you're working in a café," Laure said. "I'd stay away from the office too. What about Gilles's autopsy? Did they get anything they can use from that?"

"Nothing. He'll be buried soon, but they're waiting for some extended family members who live abroad."

Jean-Philippe checked his phone again. "No messages, no calls." Then he looked Laure in the eye. "Now that I've given you what I have, I repeat my question: how did you know about the label?"

"I got it straight from a dead chef's mouth."

28

It was impossible to leave Lyon without stopping at the Café des Fédérations. Yves Rivoiron would be a key figure in her coverage of the city's food scene, and Laure told Paco that she intended to spend her last evening at his restaurant on the Rue Major Martin, near the town hall. Of course, Paco had to go along, not only to take the photos, but also to experience the atmosphere and flavors of this *haut lieu* of Lyon gastronomy.

Rivoiron cheek-kissed Laure effusively when they arrived, wanted to know if she had come to his place to put on some weight finally, and had another table for two moved to the front of the restaurant. He then ushered his honored guests to their spot, where they could be seen by everyone. Far from being embarrassed, Laure laughed and gave a faux bow like royalty.

"What can I get you, beautiful?" Rivoiron asked.

"As always, you decide, and it will be perfect."

"And for this young man?"

Paco asked for the menu, but with a flick of her hand, Laure signaled that he should leave it up to the chef. Rivoiron had already returned to the kitchen without paying Paco any mind. Meanwhile, the waitress had brought them some Morgon in a jug, along with water.

Laure filled their glasses, and Paco watched as she began to relax. Laure ran her hand through her hair and gently pulled down the sleeves of her dark-gray cashmere sweater, a perfect backdrop for her double-strand necklace of small red beads and fine silver links. She looked lovely.

Not wanting to spoil the pleasant ambience, Paco intended to use his Leica to snap his photos. He didn't want to feel like he was on the job, not after making the effort to dress in his best black shirt, which he had pulled crumpled from his backpack and carefully steamed in the shower, and splash on a scent he used only on special occasions. The saleswoman who had suggested the cologne described it as woody, with notes of bergamot and blackcurrant leaves, which was good enough for him.

The restaurant would be almost romantic, he thought, if it weren't for the pigs. Their images were everywhere, inside and out. There was even a mural of a pig reading a newspaper on a toilet.

Still, he was feeling like a lucky man, He had the privilege of sharing a fulfilling dining experience with this charming, elegant, and lively woman, while Jean-Philippe had nothing to show for his little tête-à-tête at the café. He had been tempted to ask Laure what they had talked about, as he was curious about the latest murder too, but he had decided against it.

The festivities opened with an assortment of pork offerings, including a pork and beef sausage, a creamy lentil dish called caviar of the Croix Rousse, and herring *rillettes*. Then their main courses arrived: a pike quenelle casserole with Nantua sauce for Laure, whose eyes lit up, and a big plate of tripe for Paco, who panicked.

This had been Yves Rivoiron's decision. His choice was daring and could have been provocative, but it proved to be more of a revelation. With his first bite, Paco's apprehension transformed into ecstasy.

"My, Paco, get hold of yourself," Laure said. "Have you never tasted tripe before?"

"Just the thought has always sickened me. But this is sublime!"

Laura motioned to the chef, who was watching a short distance away.

"What a risky choice," Paco said, grinning. "This is the first time I've had tripe, and I'm so glad you made it for me. I love it!"

"Hallelujah, a tripe virgin!" Rivoiron said, turning from Paco to Laure. "I knew just by the sight of him."

"At home, they cook it with tomato, and it looks disgusting," Paco said. "But frankly…"

"There are plenty of ways to prepare tripe. Every country has a different version. What you've got on your plate is the real tripes à la lyonnaise."

"Is it hard to make?"

"The key is soaking the tripe in cold water for a whole day. You must change the water regularly. Then you blanch and drain it. Meanwhile, you prepare a broth with vegetables and a bouquet garni. With a sharp knife, you cut the tripe into thin strips and cook the strips in the broth for at least two and a half hours. Then you drain them."

"That doesn't sound too difficult, but it's time-consuming."

"Ah, but we're not done yet, young man! Next, you slice eight large white onions and toss them in a skillet with a pat of butter and a little oil. Cook them until they're soft but not brown. Add the tripe and brown it, seasoning with salt. You'll want it crispy. Arrange the tripe on a dish. Deglaze the pan with red vinegar, and pour the liquid over the tripe. Sprinkle with chopped parsley, and there you have it."

The meal ended just as happily, with praline pies that evoked happy childhood memories. Paco snapped some pictures while Laure asked for the bill.

"We're not going to be friends if you insist on paying for your meal," the waitress said with a large smile.

"Ah, but I must pay for it," Laure said, returning her smile. "My magazine insists."

Rivoiron, who was aligning stemware on a shelf behind the bar, stepped in. "For once, could you allow us to feed you for the sheer pleasure of it?"

"I'm so sorry," Laure answered. "I cannot. But our evening with you has been divine, and I look forward to the next time. Meanwhile, be careful. Don't close up alone while that killer is on the loose."

The waitress pulled out a long kitchen knife from behind the counter and waved it. "Just let him try!"

Her aggressive come-on seemed to surprise Rivoiron, who wasted no time joining in the spirit. He threw his towel on the counter and reached for a huge rosette sausage hanging from a beam. "And I'll stick this where he'll remember it," he shouted, swinging it in the air.

29

On her way to breakfast at the hotel, Laure followed a gray-haired couple down the hallway and stairs. They spoke English with an American accent, but it could just as well have been German, Spanish, or some other European language. The hotel was full of tourists eager to experience the famed city where Paul Bocuse made his living and home.

Laure was thinking about everything she had to do on her last day in Lyon when she entered the dining room, where a waitress was busy restocking cups and cutlery for the continental breakfast buffet. Laure scanned the room, looking for a free table, and spotted Jean-Philippe, who rose and beckoned her to join him.

"What are you doing here?" she asked.

Jean-Philippe frowned. "You don't look so happy to see me."

"No, not at all. I'm sorry. I'm just afraid you've come with bad news. Was there another murder last night?"

"No, at least not that I'm aware of. I'm here because the police have a lead."

Laure nodded. "Let me get some breakfast, and I'm all yours." She returned with scrambled eggs and thin slices of aromatic smoked salmon. She put down her plate, took her seat, and gave Jean-Philippe her full attention.

"The police combed every corner of Les Vieux Sarments. Of course, they found thousands of fingerprints. Nothing surprising there. But they say Chevrion tried to defend himself, and in the struggle the murderer left behind evidence."

"Traces of DNA?"

"I don't believe so. But I did manage to squeeze some information out of the forensics lab. Don't ask me to reveal my source."

"I would never do that."

"The lab rats worked all night. The brass is getting antsy, and nobody wants these homicides to influence the upcoming elections. Anyway, this morning I heard they found some blood…"

Laure didn't wait for him to finish. "From the murderer?"

"No, it was animal blood. It had been heated—cooked, if you prefer."

"What animal?"

"I don't know. They also found plant matter, fiber, and starch. I don't know any more. But I was able to get my hands on something. It's confidential. I shouldn't have this, let alone share it, but for you..."

Jean-Philippe didn't finish his sentence. He stared hungrily at Laure. Had he forgotten why he was there? She didn't mind the attention, but could he get on with it?

After nearly a minute of unbearable silence, during which Laure stared back as impassively as she could, he pulled a sheet of paper from his pocket, unfolded it, and handed it over.

Jean-Philippe cleared his throat. "I thought you might be able to help. They found traces of these herbs and spices on Chevrion's clothing. The police searched the restaurant and reviewed each of the dishes on his menu. It seems that none include the ingredients. Can you corroborate that?"

Laure read and reread the list, moving her finger down the sheet.

"I can corroborate," she said. "I know Chevrion's kitchen. I have no doubt. The cops don't need to waste their time searching his place anymore." She looked up from the list. "I see you put plus signs in front of the first four ingredients. What are they for?"

"They were found in greater quantities than the others. Your input will be a big help, Laure. We may be getting somewhere!"

He pulled out his cell phone to make a call. Then he hesitated. "I have to go, Laure. You understand. Keep the list. If you have any ideas, don't hesitate to let me know. I'll call you if I have anything new. You're still interested, right?"

"Of course."

Jean-Philippe stood up and put his coat on. As he leaned over and kissed her on the cheek, whispering a final good-bye, Laure saw over his shoulder that Paco had just entered the breakfast room. Paco's eyes locked in on them, and his smile sank into a frown. He turned away quickly to get a cup of coffee. Once the reporter had left, he sat down at Laure's table and slumped over his coffee.

30

The breakfast room had emptied out. Laure and Paco were the only ones left. He was ripping his almond croissant into small pieces and tossing them in his mouth without any sign of pleasure. Laure was silently staring at the list she'd gotten from Jean-Philippe.

"Not too tired?" ventured the photographer.

"I'm okay, thanks."

"Did you actually get some rest, after your busy night?" Paco spit out.

Laure searched her purse and retrieved a notepad topped with the hotel's logo. She scribbled a few words. "My night couldn't have been quieter."

"You must have been disappointed then."

Laure looked up and sighed. "Paco, I'll pretend I didn't hear that. Right now, there are more important things to tend to. Do you know what's on this sheet of paper?"

"No," Paco muttered.

Laure quickly told him what the forensics lab had found.

"Some animal blood and fifteen herbs and spices? What are they making of it?"

"Nothing yet. Jean-Philippe brought me the list this morning. He didn't want to send it by text."

"He came this morning?"

Laure scowled. "I have the feeling you got up on the wrong side of the bed this morning. I'll pour us some more coffee." She walked over to the coffee station, and when she returned with steaming cups, she saw that Paco was smiling and sitting up straight.

"So you're saying the investigation is actually moving forward with this list of ingredients?" he asked.

"Possibly. It does make sense that the murderer would be in the same business. Maybe he's a competitor. But using the list to nail the killer could be very difficult."

"Downright impossible, I'd say."

"Not easy, but the hunt should be rather interesting. Look there, for example. They found a lot of ginger."

"So?"

"It's used in Japanese, Chinese, Indian, and Thai cuisines, but you also find it in pastries and other culinary traditions."

"That doesn't narrow the field much. What's another one?"

"Cumin. Dishes from the Indian Ocean region come to mind, but you can also find it in spiced gouda cheese from the Netherlands, and it's used in North Africa's couscous dishes. Saffron's on the list too."

"That's used in paella! My mother kept a small jar of saffron above the stove, and I wasn't allowed to touch it."

"No surprise there. It costs a fortune. By the way, tell your mother to store her saffron in a cool dark cupboard away from direct heat. It'll stay fresh longer."

"Trying to tell my mother how to run her kitchen will get me in trouble, for sure!"

"Getting back to the list, saffron's found not only in paella, but also in many Central Asian, Indian, Iranian, and Middle Eastern dishes. The forensics lab came up with traces of paprika too."

"I also know about paprika! It's in chorizo."

"Indeed, it's used quite a bit in Spain," Laura said. "In *filetes de lomo* and mussel *escabeche*, but perhaps it's best known as a Hungarian goulash ingredient."

"Never tried it. The word 'goulash' turns me off."

"You don't know what you're missing, Paco. I'll give you the name of a restaurant in Paris where you can get a great goulash. You'll change your mind."

Paco looked over at the paper. "What else is on that list of yours?"

"Nutmeg. It's used in béchamel sauce, potato gratin, and quiche Lorraine. It's rather ordinary. You can even find it in some colas."

"Okay, so much for our world tour of food. What we must do now is figure out what dish— or dishes—include all of the spices and herbs. Correct?"

"That's what I'm thinking. And to complicate matters, we don't know anything specific about the quantities. Cloves are on the list, but you don't use the same amount in gingerbread as you use in *pot-au-feu*, sauerkraut, curries, cookies, and some African dishes."

"Or for a toothache! My grandmother made me—"

"Wait a minute," Laure interrupted as she quickly went down the page and starred some of the items. "You may be onto something. Several of the spices are used in medicinal treatments too. That's the case with these four, for sure. Unless..."

Pencil in hand, Laure turned over the sheet of paper and drew six columns. She started putting the main ingredients—ginger, cumin, saffron, and so on—in the columns. Then she arranged the other ingredients, making sure to consult the list on the other side of the paper. She tried all possible combinations, mixing two columns, adding another, and going back and reworking them.

"Unless what?" Paco finally asked.

Laura looked up at him. "Follow me!"

31

Laure rushed into the first bookstore they found and bought a guide to Lyon's two hundred hidden passageways, with photos, maps, comments, and annotations. She barged out the door and raced across the Palais de Justice footbridge, with Paco on her heels.

"Slow down," he called out. "How can you go so fast in those shoes?"

Shortening her stride, she started telling him about the traboules. "These private passages are one of Lyon's most fascinating features. They date from the Renaissance and were built for convenience. The silk workers from the Croix Rousse used them to haul rolls of fabric from one building to another."

Paco's labored breathing had returned to normal. "I know about them. They were used by journeymen and other workers too. I read that the smell in the traboules could get pretty ripe back then. Sanitation wasn't all that great."

Laure nodded. "The French Resistance used the traboules during World War II. Drove the Germans crazy. They're a real labyrinth, perfect for shortcuts, secret meetings, and message drops."

On the right bank, they speed walked along the pier and stopped at No. 10, near the Cèdre Bleu, a Lebanese restaurant.

"Do you have a stopwatch function on your cell phone?" Laure asked.

"Yep."

"And you know how to use it?"

"Of course!" Paco took out his phone and pressed the icon. "All right, I'm ready."

"I go first. I open the doors, and you time it."

"*¡Adelante!* Go for it!"

They made time, following a long tiled corridor and turning left. After about fifteen meters, they took a stone staircase and strode through a short hallway before rushing down more steps leading to another hallway that brought them to the gates overlooking the Place du Governement.

"Stop! How long?"

"Thirty-two seconds."

"Let's cross the square to the next door. She walked quickly to 10 Rue Saint Jean, near a bouchon called Les Chandelles, and stopped in front of a heavy varnished door.

"How long?"

"Thirteen seconds."

"Perfect. Here we go again."

With Paco close behind, Laure took a dark passageway that rose slightly midcourse until they reached the Place du Petit College between the Rue du Boeuf and the Rue de Gadagne.

"Twenty-one seconds."

"How much altogether?"

"Well, thirty-two, plus thirteen, plus twenty-one—that makes sixty-six seconds."

"One minute, six seconds," she repeated. She took a few deep breaths to re-energize and reached for the brass door handle. "Now we do it the other way."

"Are you sure?"

"Absolutely. But this time we don't stop on the square, and we keep the clock going to the quay."

They completed the return trip in one minute, two seconds.

"Less time because we knew the route and didn't hesitate," Laure said. "The time difference is almost imperceptible, but it could make a difference. Someone who knows these passageways could get where he's going in less than a minute."

"Quite possible. So now will you explain?"

"I have to check something else. Let's try an alternative route without using the passages. We'll go around the block and head toward the Gadagne Museum. I found the shortest way on the map. Let's do that at a good clip. You time it."

They strode along the quay to the Rue de la Baleine, following it to the square bearing the same name, where they took the Rue Saint Jean. After five meters, they veered left to the tiny Rue Tramassac, finally reaching the Place du Petit College.

"What's the verdict?" Laure asked.

"Two minutes, three seconds, but let's not nitpick!"

Laure was having a hard time containing her excitement. "Okay, we'll say it's about two minutes if you take the usual route, provided you hurry."

"Will you tell me now what this is all about?"

"That's two times longer. Four minutes instead of two. Forgive me, Paco, but if I tell you why we just did all that, you'll think I'm crazy!"

32

Cecile opened the door, a surprised look on her face.

"Laure, I wasn't expecting you," she said, not budging from her spot. "I thought you'd be out of town by now."

Laure waited to be let in. "Yes, I will be going back to Paris shortly, but I wanted to stop by first."

"All right, then, come in." Cecile opened the door all the way and stepped back. "I do have to leave in a few minutes, though. François is coming by to pick me up. He has a doctor's appointment, and I want to go with him. He might need knee surgery, and that would mean I'd be spending more time at the store. But we have time to talk. Let me heat up some water for tea."

Laure followed Cecile through the living room, with its three tall windows, linen-covered furniture, and sustainable table into the roomy white-washed kitchen. It smelled of disinfectant and polish.

She watched as Cecile put the water on her six-burner commercial gas range, which she had insisted on when they moved into their apartment. It wouldn't do for the owners of a tableware store to have anything less than the best in the heart of their home.

"So, tell me, what brings you here?" Cecile asked, opening a cupboard and pulling out two porcelain cups.

"It's the tagine you prepared for us the other night," Laure said. "I loved it, and I was wondering if I could have the recipe. I'd like to try it myself and maybe use it in the magazine."

Cecile's cheeks flushed. "Of course, you can have the recipe. But you didn't need to come in person to get it. I would have been happy to e-mail it. In fact, why don't I do that? Then we can just sit down and chat a bit."

She started pulling out a stool from the island.

"Actually, Cecile, I'd prefer getting the recipe now, if you don't mind."

Cecile opened the island's top drawer. She reached in and produced a sheet of paper.

"Here it is," she said, laying it on the veined-marble counter. "Let me copy the recipe for you."

Laure stepped closer. "Could I look at it first?"

Cecile slid the paper in Laure's direction.

Laure leaned over it and then turned her attention back to Cecile. "I had no idea the recipe called for that many spices."

"It is a sophisticated dish," Cecile said. She went silent for a moment before looking Laure in the eye. "But you already knew that, didn't you? Now tell me why you're really here."

The water on the range was coming to a boil, and Laure could feel the heat from the burner. She took a deep breath. "All right, Cecile. Traces of some spices and food were found at Eric Chevrion's restaurant. They matched the ingredients in this recipe."

Cecile's folded her arms. "That doesn't mean anything, Laure. He was a chef. He must have used those ingredients all the time."

"In fact, he didn't. He didn't cook with those exact spices."

"Still, Laure, don't you think this is a little far-fetched? We were all together the night Eric was murdered. Remember? We had dinner and watched the soccer game after I cleaned up the mess your Spanish assistant made. No way could I have been in two places at the same time. Besides, why in the world would I want to kill Eric? He was my brother's friend."

"You're so right, Cecile. You couldn't be in two places at the same time. But you weren't where we thought you were—were you? And you did have a reason for killing Eric. But let's not get into all of that right now. I want to talk about your brother and Gilles and Eric. They were friends, right?"

"Yes."

"All this time I'd been thinking the only thing they had in common were their bonds from childhood and their careers. But I was wrong. They had something else in common." Laure waited for Cecile to ask her what it was, but the woman was just staring at her, refusing to take the bait.

"Then I'll tell you what they had in common: sisters. Remember the day I came over to extend my condolences? You were here with Nathalie Chevrion and Veronique Mandrin. You told me you were old friends. 'We go way back,' if I recall correctly."

Cecile continued to stare at her. "Go on, then."

"Cecile, after your father died, your mother gave the family restaurant to Jerome, didn't she? You've always taken great pride in your cooking. I bet that hurt like hell—your mother choosing your brother over you. After all, Lyon's great bouchons got their start as woman-owned ventures. By all rights, you thought the restaurant should be yours. You had worked in the restaurant as a child, just like your brother. Jerome was even younger than you. What an injustice!"

Laure watched as Cecile unfolded her arms and clenched her fists. Anger flashed in her eyes. "Yes, that restaurant should have been mine. Are you happy now? Do you really think I was satisfied with selling plates and bowls in that silly store when I was just as good—if not better—in the kitchen than my brother? And to think my mother betrayed me that way! She knew I wanted the restaurant. I had earned it!"

"And Nathalie and Veronique should have inherited their family restaurants too. Am I correct?"

The tea kettle let out a piercing whistle. The two women ignored it.

"Yes, you're right. We were cheated. But we moved past it. We'll just leave it at that. Now go. Get out of here!"

"I'm sorry, Cecile. We can't leave it at that. You know what you did. We're calling the police."

"No, we're not!" Cecile shouted, her facial muscles twitching. She took a step toward Laure, and it was then that Laure spotted the rolling pin on the counter, no more than an inch from Cecile's fingers. The woman picked it up and hoisted it in the air, ready to swing.

Laure's response was instinctive. She blocked the rolling pin with her left forearm. She grabbed Cecile's shoulder with her right hand and pulled her close. Then she swept her leg behind Cecile's and forced her to the tile floor. She followed up with a punch to Cecile's chest.

Cecile lay stunned before catching her breath.

Just as Laure was rising to her feet, François burst into the kitchen.

"My God, what have you done to her," he shouted, rushing over to Cecile. He cradled her in his arms as she began to sob.

"Your wife has something to tell you, François. But first we've got to call the police."

33

At regular intervals, a monotonous recording delivered the offerings in car No. 2. "We remind you that the bar has a wide selection of tasty and nutritious meals, sandwiches, salads, and desserts, along with an assortment of hot and cold beverages."

"How nice of you. Thank you, Paco," Laure said, accepting the cup of tea he had brought back to their seats. "What did you select? I'm guessing they didn't have tripe."

"Unfortunately not! This was the only thing that looked halfway decent."

Paco unwrapped the package, revealing two slices of soft bread. Laure couldn't see what was inside.

He took a bite and made a face. "Crappy ham, a pickle that's too vinegary, limp lettuce leaf, mayonnaise that smells so sweet—my stomach's turning—and two slices of polystyrene. I let my appetite get the better of me. I should have waited until we got to Paris."

"Sorry I took so long. I was afraid we'd miss the train altogether and wanted to warn you. Honestly, I didn't think I'd need that much time."

"I thought it was rather quick, as good-byes go, and even a bit chilly. But hey, that's just me. There's no place more romantic than the platform of a train station."

Laure ignored the comment and continued. "I owe you an explanation, Paco. It all came together this morning, after we got that list of spices. I couldn't stop thinking about them, and then everything just clicked. I remembered things and put two and two together—or rather, one plus two. But if it hadn't been for the list, the murders would still be unsolved. I couldn't leave without seeing Jean-Philippe. The least he deserved was the whole story, and he wasn't going to get that from the police."

"Very collegial of you," Paco said.

"The story won't be in our magazine anyway," Laure answered.

Actually, Jean-Philippe hadn't been chilly at all when they parted on the station platform. He had apologized for the time they had lost between their first romantic encounter and their dinner in Lyon.

"I remember that sweet day we spent together, and I was so foolish to let my work get the better of me," he had told her. "I won't let that happen again. Maybe I'll start looking for a job in Paris. *Le Monde* might be interested in hiring a seasoned crime reporter."

Laure had almost grimaced. Certainly, his lack of ardor after their initial fling had thrown her off—it was hardly what she was used to. But she wasn't interested in a serious relationship. She was fine with him staying in Lyon.

"If you want to move to a better job at a bigger paper, I'm all for it," she had told him. "But please, don't move to Paris for me."

Laure felt a twinge of guilt when she saw the disappointed look on Jean-Philippe's face. She moved to soothe his bruised ego. "But that doesn't mean we can't see each other from time to time and enjoy each other's company. Remember, I still owe you that dinner."

"And I intend to take you up on that," he had said with a bittersweet smile before kissing her good-bye."

Laure turned her attention to Paco and resumed her story. "It seems so obvious now that the spice road would lead to Cecile."

"Jerome's own sister." Paco threw the remains of his sandwich into the small trash receptacle. "The same Cecile who had us over for dinner."

"Exactly! And I have to give you some credit too, Paco. You got me thinking when you mentioned the medicinal use of spices. I started looking at the list from a different perspective, from the perspective of blends. I don't know why it took so long. *Ras el hanout*, the North African spice mix, matched, at least one that's sold in the supermarket. There's also a curry blend, and that's when I remembered Cecile's tagine. It contained both, along with ginger, cumin, and saffron."

"Nice deduction, but that hardly proved Cecile was a murderer."

"You're right. But I had additional information. The forensics analysis also revealed traces of starch. The vegetables in the tagine included…"

Paco cut in. "Potatoes!"

"Yes, and there were vegetable fibers too. I guessed it had to be traces of zucchini or carrot, and we had animal blood."

"The lamb!"

"All that ended up on Chevrion's clothes, as it did on Cecile's pants after you did your master-server number on her. And I've been meaning to tell you: I don't think the turmeric stain will come out of your pants. But take them to a good dry cleaner, and that might do the trick."

"Doesn't make any difference now," Paco responded, "I threw them out. So here I assumed she was angry about me getting tagine all over her pants and breaking one of her good dishes." Paco opened the packet of chocolate-covered shortbread cookies he had bought along with the sandwich. "You're thinking the sauce on Cecile's pants got on Chevrion when she killed him, probably during the struggle."

"Yes."

Paco, a doubtful look on his face, offered Laure a cookie.

She shook her head. The tea was enough.

"I understand your reasoning about the spices," Paco said. "There's something that doesn't fit, though. Cecile spent the whole evening with us. She couldn't be in two places at the same time."

"You're right, but there was one giveaway. Didn't you find anything strange about the dessert?"

"It was excellent."

"It was good. But what about the speculoos cookies she used as the base of each mousse? Did you notice anything about them?"

"Yes, they were delicious. So?"

"They were soggy. She said she was going into the kitchen to finish her dessert. That's when she should have been in the kitchen unmolding the domes on the individual layers of speculoos cookies and drizzling them with the mocha sauce. Last-minute preparation ensures constrasting textures between the sauce, the mousse, and the crisp cookie base. But, there was none of that in Cecile's creation. Her speculoos were soft and limp. She'd prepared the desserts well ahead of time."

"I'm not sure I'm following."

"Remember? Cecile asked us to leave her alone. She wanted fifteen minutes of peace and quiet to finish the dessert. But the dessert was already finished. She didn't need to be in the kitchen."

"So she wasn't in the kitchen?"

"No, Paco She wasn't in the kitchen."

Laure lifted the tea to her lips. Her hand was trembling. She was doing her best to cover her feelings, but in fact, the face off with Cecile had unnerved her. She had always admired Cecile and been so fond of her. She still had a hard time believing that Cecile could actually murder someone.

And then there was the news Jean-Philippe had shared on the station platform before their goodbye. François had suffered a heart attack less than an hour after his wife's arrest. The paramedics had arrived in the nick of time.

Laure recalled a quote by German philosopher Friedrich Shiller. "Revenge is barren of itself; it is the dreadful food it feeds on; its delight is murder, and its end is despair."

Laure shook her head and put her cup down. "Another clue: I'm not a fan of that dessert. There was no reason she'd think I was. And she made such a big deal of saying it was something she had prepared especially for me."

"But Laure, we're talking about a very quick turnaround. It seems impossible to do all that in just fifteen minutes. Unless..."

"You take the shortcut. That's why we timed the route through the hidden passageways. It's because of Jean-Philippe that I thought of them. Do you remember when I met up with him after we returned from Bourg-en-Bresse?"

"I remember it very well."

"I was surprised to see him join us so fast, and I understood only after we took two of the passageways together. With the guide, I found the traboule closest to the building where Cecile lives. Using the shortcut, she had enough time to go kill Eric Chevrion and come back and serve us dessert."

"Coming in singing with tears in her eyes. I remember that very well. Still, some pieces are missing. What was her motive for murdering Chevrion? And she couldn't have committed the first two murders. She was visiting friends with her husband when her brother was killed, and the next day, when Mandrin was murdered, they were at the opera, stuck in their seats."

"You're right, Paco. It's a long and complicated story. And I'm sure Jean-Philippe will do it justice."

34

The spread on Lyon's bouchons met Laure's standards. On the computer at her desk, she scanned the layout, scrutinizing every detail and appreciating the overall balance, along with Paco's photographs, which would reproduce impeccably. She clicked back to the main story and reread it.

"Nice job of editing this," she said, turning to Daphne, who was looking over her shoulder. "And good catch on that black truffle in the pistachio sausage. I don't know how I could have left it out."

"That's why every piece of copy needs a second pair of eyes," Daphne said. "Even the managing editor's."

"So right you are. We should make it to press with no problems, unlike the last issue. Thank God everything came together."

"In fact, we're almost ahead of schedule. You just need to get your Editor's Corner column to me before the end of the week. You usually have it done earlier than this."

Laure looked up at Daphne, whose hair was now tinged with purple. "I know. It's just that this Lyon stuff has really gotten to me. I love being a journalist, but I never wanted to be a crime reporter! By the way, I like your hair."

Daphne patted her tresses. "Thanks. I sent you an article from a freelancer on Normandy's cider producers and farmers. Tell me what you think."

"Will do, but maybe we should hold onto it. It'll be more timely before next year's apple harvest. We'll just have to make sure nobody's gone out of business. Speaking of business—how's your side job coming along? I loved your CD. Have you gotten any gigs?"

"As a matter of fact, we have. A club in Lyon has booked us for December."

"That's terrific, Daphne. Amandine and I will be there, front and center. I'm sure Paco will tag along too."

"Sounds like a plan." Daphne gathered her papers and left the office, giving Laure a chance to check her e-mails, where she found what she had been waiting for.

"My dearest Laure, I'm sending you the article that I couldn't have written, if it weren't for you. Without your excellent sleuthing skills, the investigation would still be at a standstill. If you ever tire of working for magazines, I'm sure you could have a thriving career as a private investigator. Don't forget that you owe me that second dinner at La Mère Brazier when you come back. Yours, J-P."

35

A LONG-SIMMERING STEW OF SIBLING RIVALRY - BY JEAN-PHILIPPE RAMEAU

Three chefs—Jerome Thevenay, Gilles Mandrin, and Eric Chevrion—murdered after hours in their kitchens. The homicide scenes were grisly. The chefs were trussed like the whole chickens they prepared every night. Their heads were stuffed in bags. Was this the work of a jealous competitor, a wise guy who wanted their businesses, or maybe even a serial killer?

As it turned out, the killer wasn't any of them, and the killer wasn't one person. There were three killers, in fact. And they were all blood relatives of the victims.

—Véronique Lafarqeau, born Mandrin, was a stay-at-home mother who occasionally handled her husband's accounts at the family hardware store. All her neighbors liked her, pointing out that she home-schooled her children.

—Nathalie Chevrion, whom some called a social worker with a big heart, shared a sweet life with
her companion, a technician for a petrochemical
plant near Villeurbanne, and their fifteen-year-old
daughter. In the winter, she passed out blankets to
the homeless, and in the summer, she canned vegetables for the food pantry at her church.

—Cecile Frangier, born Thevenay, had a
thriving shop on the Rue Grenette, a former
knife-making venture, which she and her husband,
François, had converted to a trendy retail business
devoted to the arts of the table. Her store's china
and napkins were often featured in newspaper
articles.

Three women who were admired and accomplished. But beneath the veneer of respectability,
all of them harbored a sense of loss seasoned with
toxic resentment. Their brothers had taken over
their family restaurants, which had been estab-
lished generations earlier by their female forebears,
Lyon mothers. Cheated of their inheritances for
reasons they considered chauvinistic, even misog-
ynistic, they nurtured a bitterness that finally came
to a head.

A MACABRE RECIPE

Lyon's a city of half a million people, but in
many ways, it's a small town. And the restaurant
community is tight. It made sense that even though
the women led disparate lives, they would know

each other. In fact, they had been childhood friends. And, as it happened, they had developed a strong bond, based on their mutual resentment. Eventually, conversations that had once ended with "it's not fair" became strategizing sessions. The women were bent on taking back what was theirs.

They came up with a Machiavellian plan: to kill the three brothers in quick succession so the murders would look like the work of a serial killer. They needed an original strategy that would be perceived as the murderer's signature and wouldn't require a lot of strength. They decided to enter the premises at closing time, when staff members were gone and the boss was counting his proceeds, to hit him from behind with a rolling pin, tie him up, encase his head in a garbage bag, and simulate a robbery.

One problem remained. As jealous and angry as they were, the prospect of killing their own flesh and blood wasn't appealing. Again, they had the answer. They wouldn't murder their own brothers. They each would murder one of the other brothers. Veronique Lafarqeau began by suffocating Jerome Thevenay. Nathalie Chevrion murdered Gilles Mandrin, and Cecile Frangier ended Eric Chevrion's life. The plan had an additional advantage. The sister of each man would have an alibi for the night of her brother's death. Indeed, the police had cleared family members because numerous witnesses had placed them elsewhere.

ONE INGREDIENT TOO MANY

The plan went well until Cecile Frangier made a fatal mistake. She went to Les Vieux Sarments with pants freshly stained with a sauce containing various spices, none of which were in the restaurant kitchen.

During questioning, Frangier confessed that she had experienced a change of heart. The confrontation with the reality of death and the police investigation had shaken her resolve. But her accomplices, who had carried their weight, pressured her to go through with it. Worried, Frangier wanted to be especially careful when she committed the murder she had agreed to. She chose the night of a soccer match, as she was familiar with the bouchon tradition of closing early so staff members could watch the kick-off. In addition, she decided to take the passageways of the traboules near her home, which shortened the time needed to carry out her assignment. Having invited friends to dinner at her home, she excused herself for fifteen minutes to finish a dessert, which, in fact, had been prepared earlier in the day. Then she held up her end of the devil's bargain.

Asked why she had changed the MO, Frangier explained that anger had compounded her anxiety. A dinner guest had broken a dish inherited from her grandmother. She had lost her temper and forgotten to wear gloves when she grabbed the rope and plastic bag. Concerned about leaving traces of her DNA on the victim, she decided to use what was on hand in the kitchen: heavy kitchen twine, a freezer bag, and her own rolling pin.

Editor's note: This case might never have been solved, were it not for the contribution of Laure Grenadier, managing editor of *Plaisirs de Table*, whose skill and fine palate led to the arrest of the three women. An issue of her magazine devoted to Lyon's bouchons will hit the stands in December.

Laure shivered. Cecile had tried to bash her skull in with the same rolling pin. She didn't want to think of the end she could have met if she hadn't been quick with her arms and feet.

She picked up her phone to call Jean-Philippe to thank him for the recognition and perhaps see if he'd be free for dinner the following weekend.

But then she thought better of it. Instead, she entered Amandine's number. "Hi sweetheart, I just had an idea. You've been thinking about going meatless, and I've had enough sausage, veal, and poached chicken to last me awhile. Let's splurge and treat ourselves to the vegetable tasting menu at L'Arpège, near the Musée Rodin. The meal should be a masterpiece."

Thank you for reading
Minced, Marinated, and Murdered

Please share your thoughts and reactions on your favorite social media and retail platforms.

If you enjoyed this story, please consider reading

THE WINEMAKER DETECTIVE SERIES

Also by Noël Balen, with Jean-Pierre Alaux. This fun made-for-TV mystery series takes readers deep into French wine country.

Treachery in Bordeaux
Grand Cru Heist
Nightmare in Burgundy
Deadly Tasting
Cognac Conspiracies
Mayhem in Margaux
Flambé in Armagnacontmartre Mysteries
Backstabbing in Beaujolais
Late Harvest Havoc
Tainted Tokay
Red-Handed in Romanée-Conti
Requiem in Yquem

www.lefrenchbook.com/winemaker-detective-series/